OLIVER NOCTURNE

BLOOD
TIES

KEVIN EMERSON

SCHOLASTIC INC.

NEW YORK   TORONTO   LONDON   AUCKLAND   SYDNEY
MEXICO CITY   NEW DELHI   HONG KONG   BUENOS AIRES

ISBN-13: 978-0-545-05803-2
ISBN-10: 0-545-05803-1

Text copyright © 2008 by Kevin Emerson.
Illustrations copyright © 2008 by Scholastic Inc.
SCHOLASTIC, APPLE, and associated logos are trademarks and/or registered trademarks of Scholastic Inc.

12 11 10 9 8 7 6 5 4 3 2   9 10 11 12 13/0

Printed in the U.S.A.   40
First printing, November 2008

Contents

Contents

For the 826 readers: K.O., L.C., D.W., and O.L. (who knew Lythia before I did)...

Prologue

The Vandenburg Research Station, located at Prydz Bay on the continent of Antarctica, near the magnetic South Pole of the planet, was a lovely place to spend the month of June if you didn't mind extreme cold or near total darkness.

Professor Darren Stevens was one of those rare people who found the icy desolation of an Antarctic winter peaceful and relaxing. Watching the sun just edging over the rim of the frozen sea gave him a feeling of relief. He was glad to be so far from the violence and struggles of the rest of the world. Here, all he had to worry about was the stinging wind, the endless ice, and his geologic instruments.

Day after day, Professor Stevens sat at his computer, his face bathed in blue light from the monitor, holding his coffee mug with the faded words I SAW MER-MAIDS AT WEEKI WACHEE SPRINGS barely visible across the white porcelain, and studied the graphs of his ice core samples. The long tubes of ice were striped with tiny layers of dust and dead microscopic creatures. Just a few inches told a million years of history: the global warmings and ice ages, the rise and fall of species and civilizations. It made him smirk at the troubles and pain of the people up north in the sunlight. Didn't they know that their entire lives would only add up to a layer of dust thinner than a fingernail?

Studying the ice cores soothed the professor for another reason. People were going crazy about the health of the earth these days, but the ice cores proved that there was no need to worry. It wasn't like the world was going to end or anything. No matter how human beings mucked up the planet, in time it would fix itself, adapting and changing, layer by layer. And so the professor could sit here in the cold, quiet night without any worry. . . .

❋

Unfortunately for the professor, there were other beings that enjoyed the dark and didn't mind the cold too much. One of them was standing in front of him now.

"What are Hannah's favorite toys?" the young vampire girl named Lythia LeRoux asked. She gazed at the professor kindly. When he didn't reply, Lythia answered her own question, as she enjoyed doing. "I bet she likes horses. Little human girls always like horses. Who knows why. . . . Their blood tastes terrible." Lythia sighed. "And what is her favorite food?"

Again, when the professor didn't reply, Lythia did. "I bet she likes brownies. And probably lots of those wicked foods, like pizza and macaroni and cheese." Lythia wrinkled her nose playfully. Like most vampires, she absolutely hated cheese. She blew her magenta hair out of her eyes and took a bite of the frozen candy bar she held in her red-mittened hand. The chocolate cracked like ice, and Lythia scowled.

For a moment, her lavender eyes narrowed at the professor. "You know . . ." She stepped closer, lowering her voice. "I can't wait to get out of here — all this nasty ice — but my father says it won't be much longer now. And until then, at least we can be friends, right?"

Professor Stevens didn't reply, as usual, but his eyes did seem to momentarily flicker with life. This made Lythia smile, though she knew that she'd probably just imagined the professor's response. He was, after all, currently hanging by his armpits in a large freezer unit, his body sprinkled with frost, his skin a delicate shade of blue. He was wearing his heavy parka, the thick fur of his hood frozen around his head and stuck to his shaggy gray hair.

On either side of the professor were his beautiful three-foot-long ice-core samples. Lythia thought they looked like chimes. She'd even hit one to see if it made a pretty tone, but it had simply shattered.

"My father says that your research is pure folly," Lythia said to the professor, curling a lock of her hair around her pointed green fingernail. "He says a human trying to understand the universe is like a plankton trying to understand the ocean. . . ." She trailed off. Her father, Malcolm LeRoux, had said so very much more on the subject, going on and on, but Lythia found all that talk incredibly boring.

She looked down at her hands, where she held the professor's wallet open to the picture of his daughter, Hannah. She looked back up to the professor and his frost-speckled eyes. "I bet she tastes better than you."

Two tubes ran out of the professor's neck, snaking down to two jars on the floor. One collected a slow flow of the professor's blood, while the other added a special plasma called Sanguinaise back into the professor's system. Sanguinaise sped the process of blood regeneration. It was used when humans were put into Staesys, or frozen in time, so that when the humans woke up they wouldn't know they'd been fed on.

It was also helpful for vampires whose food supply was limited, such as if you were in Antarctica and had only one human to feed you for a week. In this case, instead of being frozen in time, the professor was literally frozen, to keep him fresh.

Sanguinaise wouldn't work forever. After a while, it would exhaust all the bone marrow in the human and cause skeletal breakdown. But Lythia didn't need to worry about that. She and her companions wouldn't be here much longer.

"Does Hannah ever have nightmares? What are they about? I love nightmares —"

"Lythia!"

Lythia spun to find her father storming into the room. Malcolm was very tall and broad, and had to hunch and twist to maneuver through the research station's cramped halls, which put him in a foul mood. He reached out and slammed the clear door on the freezing unit as he hurried by. Lythia thought she saw a flicker of disappointment in the professor's eyes. How bored he must be when she wasn't talking to him.

Malcolm continued out of the lab, ducking through a metal hatchway. "I told you," he barked over his shoulder, "the food will spoil if you keep that door open."

Lythia naturally fell into step behind her father. If he was rushing, then there was something worth rushing for. She followed him down a narrow hallway. Tiny portal windows looked out on windswept miles of silver ice and purple sky.

The hall led to another cramped room, this one lined wall to wall with computer machinery and reverberating with a shrill beeping sound. A green light blinked by a keyboard in the center of a long desk. Malcolm slapped at the keys. Monitors flickered to life and a myriad of maps appeared. Some were standard GPS, some were grid maps of the ocean floor, and there were others that rotated on multiple axes and would have made no sense to the professor or any other human. They showed the intersections of many worlds.

"Did we find it?" Lythia asked.

"I think so." Malcolm tapped quickly. "There. Yes, we've got it."

On the center monitor was a rather normal-looking map of the Indian Ocean. A red dot was blinking atop a tiny island alone on the blue sea.

"Go send a message to Ravonovich," Malcolm instructed tersely, "and let him know we've pinpointed the location where the Artifact will arrive. Tell him we'll meet him there."

Lythia turned and rushed out of the room, a spring in her step. The Artifact! It was so exciting when prophecies came true. Lythia had been lucky in her young existence to be with her dad a few times when things like this happened: when myth and possibility became reality. But none had ever been as important as this. Lythia knew that it was a big deal that her dad had finally been asked to work on the Nexia prophecy and to have his decades of Artifact research pay off. . . .

She passed through the lab and offered the professor a quick glance. "Time to run, Professor. Someone will thaw you out in time. Say hi to Hannah for me!" she said with a smile, knowing there was little chance of that.

She entered another narrow hallway, then a small living room with couches and lamps, most of which had been overturned. A bookshelf lay on the floor, its contents scattered about. There were smears of blood here and there from that other troublesome human, the professor's colleague, who had put up a fight when Lythia and her dad had arrived. He'd been taken back to their boat to sustain the crew.

Lythia picked up her shoulder bag from one of the couches, stuffing her clothes and dismembered dolls back into it. Then she turned to the wall where the bookshelf had stood. There was a tunnel carved there that dropped straight down into the ice. It had been melted using a magma drill. Lythia ducked inside and climbed down a metal ladder. At the bottom was a cylindrical cave with frozen blue walls. Another tunnel led off toward the end of the ice shelf, where their boat awaited. The tiny cave was lit by the amber glow of a swirling magmalight lantern. Beside it was a black box: a geo-harmonic phone.

Lythia touched a button on the phone and a video screen jumped to life, revealing a plush, dark office. A pointed, pale face appeared. Mr. Ravonovich cleared his throat, adjusted his bow tie, and spoke in a thin voice. "Yes, dear?"

"Father says we've got the location. He's sending it to you, and we'll meet you there."

Ravonovich nodded slowly. "Thank you, Lythia. Give your father my congratulations."

The screen flicked off.

Lythia was about to head for the boat, but she had one more thing she wanted to do. Glancing up the ladder to make sure her father wasn't coming, she reached into her shoulder bag and pulled out a flat object wrapped in crimson cloth. She carefully unfolded the fabric, revealing a diamond-shaped hand mirror with a border of jade. She held the mirror up by its short handle. Pale white light sparkled on her face, as if from many sources.

"They've found the Artifact," she whispered at the mirror.

The lights danced around, and Lythia nodded as if she was hearing a voice.

"I will," she said. She tucked the mirror back into her bag and started down the ice passage for the long journey north.

CHAPTER 1

An Uneasy Quiet

There were some things that Oliver Nocturne enjoyed about school. One was whenever Mr. VanWick was giving a history lecture and he was listening intently and no one around him was talking or snickering at him. Another was . . . well, lately that had been pretty much it. Maybe the only other thing he enjoyed about school was that today was the last day.

But the torture wasn't over yet.

Oliver was sitting on a single chair outside the door to his classroom. They'd had early dismissal, around two A.M., same as every other day during this awful month of June. The summer solstice was a week away, and the sun was so strong that even a cloudy day was dangerously bright. And because Seattle was so far north, the sun rose at nearly four in the morning and didn't set until almost ten at night. It was close to four now, and sickly dawn light was beaming into the hall from every doorway. Oliver's seat was positioned in a narrow rectangle of shadow.

The classroom door was closed. Faint murmurs echoed from inside. Oliver's parents were in there, having their parent-teacher conference with Mr. VanWick. It was the end of Oliver's fourth year of his eighth Pentath of school. A Pentath was five human years long. Since vampires aged about one year for every five human years, this meant that he was nearing the end of seventh grade. He had one more year, and then he would move on to his ninth Pentath, which was like eighth grade.

In eighth grade, all bets were off, because the moment a vampire received his demon, he graduated immediately to high school. If your demon came early, you might only spend a year in the ninth Pentath, or you could end up like Bane had, spending eight years there, until he was the only one left in his class.

High school was the promised land: no dress code, no books, no homework, just hanging out discussing the world and learning the advanced powers that only a fully demonized vampire could achieve, like Occupying animals and Evanescence, where a vampire could move as mist. There were entire lectures devoted to causing chaos, driving humans mad, corrupting governments, committing thievery and fraud, and on and on.

But all that was a long way off for Oliver. Between now and then, there was at least one more year of dress shirts and ties, textbooks and homework. Plus, Oliver wasn't sure if high school was something that his future even held. Unlike any other vampire child, he already knew who his demon was: Illisius.

Oliver knew this because he was the first in his class to have a demon dream, which signaled that your demon was on its way. In that first dream, Illisius had told Oliver that he was destined to open the Nexia Gate. Nexia was the central world of the universe. Opening the Gate would free all the vampires from Earth, allowing them to roam the higher worlds as spirits. No more sunlight or stakes or troublesome skin molds or even high school to worry about.

So what was the point of trying to do well in school, or even going? What was the point of suffering through these awful parent-teacher conferences if your destiny was to put an end to them? It made Oliver want to just get up and leave right now —

"Oliver." The door beside him had opened, and Mr. VanWick was peering out. Oliver felt a nervous twinge in his gut as he got to his feet and entered the classroom.

Large black curtains had been pulled down against the relentless early-morning light. Mr. VanWick returned to the far corner of the room. His desk was behind a folded screen for extra darkness. Oliver's parents, Phlox and Sebastian, sat before the desk, an empty chair between them. Oliver trudged toward the seat. He watched as both his parents glanced up at him, then away with barely a change in expression. They didn't look happy. Then again, when was the last time they *had* looked happy with Oliver?

"Your parents and I have been discussing," Mr. VanWick began as Oliver slumped into the empty chair, "your year. I have explained to them that despite how your studies have suffered from apparent *distractions* both in and out of school, you have compiled satisfactory marks. You've had success in history, which I have been pleased to see. And yet Ms. Estreylla reported that you rarely handed in your homework in Multi-World Math and barely passed."

Oliver shrugged. He liked history very much, actually. He thought Force Awareness and Manipulation, which was like gym class, was okay, too, except for the uniforms. Dimensional Math was just boring. And he didn't get it. He was always getting lost.

"Oliver," said Phlox, "do you have anything to say for yourself?"

"No," Oliver mumbled.

Oliver heard Sebastian shift in his chair and braced for what his father might say, but he was silent.

"I also conveyed to your parents my feeling," Mr. VanWick continued, "that despite the *events* surrounding Valentine's Day, and your social difficulties with your peers, that you have been a satisfactory participant in your Pentath, though there is room for improvement." Mr. VanWick offered what may have been a kind glance, though it was hard to make out the character of his eyes beneath his bushy eyebrows.

"Okay," said Oliver. He hadn't *felt* satisfactory since Valentine's Day, when a group known as the Brotherhood of the Fallen had used his human friend Emalie to try to slay him with sunlight. Their leader, Braiden Lang, had said that Oliver could not be allowed to open the Gate, but he hadn't said why. Oliver still didn't get that: Why would humans even care about the Gate? They barely understood their own short lives, never mind the larger universe. Most of them didn't even realize that there were vampires living among them. And for those who did, like the Brotherhood, well, why would they mind the Gate being opened? That was going to make all the vampires go away.

Saving Emalie from the Brotherhood had put an end to the short period of time during which Oliver's vampire schoolmates had thought that he was interesting and cool. Now he was considered the biggest freak in his class because he hung out with a human rather than his own kind. Nobody minded that Oliver also hung out with a zombie, Emalie's cousin Dean, because all the vampires, including his parents, thought that Oliver had killed Dean and raised him as a servant.

Only Oliver, Emalie, and Dean knew the truth: Some-one else had killed and raised Dean, someone whose identity remained a mystery.

"So . . . summer break should help," said Mr. VanWick, "and we will look forward to next year." He held a large packet of papers out over the desk.

"What's that?" Oliver asked.

Phlox reached out and took it. "This is your summer math work. We thought it would be a good idea to keep you busy."

"Have a tolerable summer," Mr. VanWick said, push-ing back from his seat and sipping from his stained goblet.

The Nocturnes walked quietly down the empty hall-way, weaving back and forth to avoid the slanting rectangles of sunlight. They took the stairs to the lower hall, headed to its end, then descended into the base-ment boiler room, where a small rusted door in a cobwebbed corner led to the sewers.

As they walked home in silence, Oliver felt none of the excitement that one might feel about being out of school for two months. Part of that had to do with the long quiet moments that he and his parents had been having, like right now. Since Valentine's Day, being around them had felt, well, uneasy. On the one hand, his parents knew about Emalie. *Get over it . . . over her,* Phlox had said. And yet Oliver had done nothing of the sort. He and Dean had been hanging out with Emalie all spring. Oliver just had to do it in secret, though for all he knew, maybe his parents knew he was still hanging out with her. They had a habit of knowing things without telling him.

On the other hand, his parents had to realize that part of the reason why Oliver was having trouble in school and hanging out with a human was their fault. He hadn't asked to be sired, which meant that he had been turned into a vampire from a human baby. Siring a child was supposed to be impossible. All the other vampire kids were made from the DNA of their parents and grown in a lab. And he hadn't asked to be created to fulfill the prophecy of opening the Nexia Gate, a fact that led people in brotherhoods to try to kill him. So in a way, wasn't anything that was weird about him really his parents' fault? Oliver felt like they had to know that, and that was part of why they were so quiet and part of why, even though they'd told him to get over Emalie, they didn't seem to be keeping that close an eye on him.

The Nocturnes reached the sewer beneath their street, passing thick wooden doors set in either side of the stone walls. There was one for each underground vampire house on Twilight Lane. Their house was number sixteen. They entered and wound up a stone spiral staircase, lit with sconces of amber magmalight, to the kitchen.

They'd just finished hanging their coats in the closet when Oliver's older brother, Bane, came bounding in from the living room.

"Did he flunk out?" Bane quipped, smirking.

"Now, Charles," Phlox warned, but her voice had none of the frustration that it used to get when Bane was harassing Oliver. Instead, as she crossed the kitchen and flicked on the plasma screen above the sink, she almost seemed to relax.

"Hello, son," said Sebastian, nodding at Bane. "Oliver's conference was fine." He headed downstairs to change.

"Boo." Bane popped open the refrigerator, grabbing a Coke. He opened a cookie jar on the counter and took out a length of candied tapeworm. His arm whipped out, and the bright red ribbon shot toward Oliver. "Think fast, bro!"

Oliver barely got his hands up in time to slap it away. He scowled. "Knock it off, foot rot!"

Bane just laughed. "Ooh, watch out." He spun and thrust his other arm, like he was throwing the Coke can —

"Whu!" Oliver cringed.

"Ha! Gotcha. Dork." Bane snapped open the can and began chugging it.

Oliver watched as, once again, Phlox said nothing. It used to be that she would scold Bane for acting this way, but Bane was the favorite son now. Was he unstable and moody? Sure, but Bane was also a real vampire, who had fought alongside his father against the Brotherhood.

"How many nights until we leave, Mom?" Bane asked.

Phlox looked up from putting away a selection of long cutting blades. "Just three, honey. I know you can wait a little longer."

"Barely," Bane scowled. "I *gotta* get out of here."

Bane was referring to their upcoming vacation. The Nocturnes had been invited by Sebastian's employer, the Half-Light Consortium, to go to Isla Necrata, an elite, invitation-only resort that always changed locations to be near a large natural phenomenon of some kind: preferably a volcanic eruption, but an earthquake or a tsunami was fine, too. Isla Necrata's location was always kept secret to insure a private resort experience, but it would no doubt be somewhere interesting. Oliver was excited about the trip — he enjoyed travel — and he couldn't imagine anywhere he could be right now that would be worse than Seattle, considering how things had been going for him.

"Destruction and devastation!" Bane cheered to himself.

"Now, Charles, just because you get to carouse with your cousins does not mean that you're going to lose control, does it?"

Bane smiled devilishly, then unleashed a mammoth belch. "Of course not, Mom."

Phlox nodded, again with all the patience in the world for Bane's antics. She sighed. "Well, at least one of us is looking forward to seeing your relatives."

They were leaving for Isla Necrata a few days early to see Phlox's extended family along the way, in the Underworld city of Morosia. It was hard to say whether that part of the trip would be any fun. It was always nice to see the grandparents. And Bane would be preoccupied with running wild and raiding human towns and such with their teenage cousins, so Oliver wouldn't have to deal with him.

But still, since Oliver didn't have a demon, he would be left behind with his parents, who would be enduring endless torment about their modern vampire ways from *their* disapproving parents. That part was kind of enjoyable to watch, because Oliver's grandparents had a pleasant double standard: On the one hand, they spoiled Oliver and treated him like the world's greatest thing, while on the other hand, they constantly criticized Phlox and Sebastian for their New World ways, even though it was *those* ways that had led to Oliver's existence. In the Old World, there were no children, only teens who had been sired and had demons. But the fun of watching his parents get treated like bad kids was tempered by the bad mood it put them in, which Oliver then had to deal with.

"Speaking of the trip," said Phlox, turning to the counter, "you should get started on this right away." She pushed the math homework toward Oliver.

"Can't it wait?" Oliver couldn't help whining a little. "Vacation just started."

"No rest for the morons!" Bane called, and ducked out of the room before Phlox could reprimand him, though Oliver doubted she even would.

"Oliver," Phlox said, her eyes on the refrigerator as she opened it and began gathering bags of pre-drained blood to make dinner. "You need to take your studies seriously." She sounded exhausted as she said it. "I'd appreciate it if you worked on this until dinner."

"Fine," Oliver muttered, taking the papers and heading into the living room. He almost wished he still had school to go to every day, if only to avoid the weirdness at home.

CHAPTER 2

Dinner's Ominous End

But not everything was going badly. One aspect of the strangeness between Oliver and his parents was working to his advantage. . . .

That evening, Oliver awoke and was dressed and up in the kitchen in moments. "I'm going out," he said as he grabbed his sweatshirt and long black raincoat from the closet.

Phlox turned from whipping cream for Belgian waffles. "Oh?" he heard her say tentatively. "And where are you going?"

Oliver started down the stairs. "Dean and I are heading to the park," he called casually over his shoulder.

Oliver could practically hear Phlox staring after him, trying to figure out what he was up to. "You should eat some breakfast."

"Not hungry," Oliver mumbled, continuing down the stairs. "Seth will be there," he added, wondering if Phlox would call sternly after him —

But she didn't. *Of course not,* Oliver thought. He popped out the door into the sewer, glad to be out of the house, but feeling annoyed that his mom hadn't even tried to stop him. What did that mean? Had his parents given up on him completely? But wasn't being left alone what he wanted? Then why did it make him feel bad?

Oliver crossed town through the sewers, making his way to a quiet street in Crown Hill. He pressed a button set in the stone wall. A manhole cover opened above him, and he leaped up into brightness. This manhole was located safely beneath a thick pine tree, but the evening light was still harsh, making him squint.

He slipped on the hood of his sweatshirt and pulled the collar of his raincoat high up over his neck. The coat was also treated with anti-insulants, which kept the heat of the summer out, so that Oliver was as cool and shaded as was possible in this miserable weather.

The street was lined with little houses, and there were humans everywhere: walking dogs, tending to flowers, throwing a Frisbee in the street. Oliver hurried up the sidewalk. He could already feel the sickly warmth through his hood and on his legs. He dodged past a small terrier that growled suspiciously, and then sprinted across a final stretch of unshaded sidewalk, leaping onto the porch of Dean's small, olive-green house. Dark curtains were pulled shut over its wide front windows.

Oliver was just reaching for the door when it flew open and a thick, meaty high school boy hurried out, slamming right into him. The boy wore a tank top and jeans and smelled all sweaty and human and horrible.

"Watch it, Sledge!" Oliver hissed, throwing back his hood and letting his eyes flare amber.

Sledge looked down at Oliver. His eyes darted about, taking in ten things at once. He was always like this, scattered and out of control. He finally saw Oliver and smiled. "Cool . . . I wish I could make my eyes do that."

"Well, we could always kill you. . . ." Oliver muttered, trying to sound ominous.

"Nice! Would you?" Sledge seemed to think this was a fine idea. "I keep asking Ms. Fitch to make me a vamp or a zombie, anything!" He frowned. "She never does it. Having some powers would be rad."

A girl's voice spoke from behind him. "Well, you've already got the power to be annoying." A tall girl with long blond hair stepped out and shoved Sledge across the porch like he was an empty cardboard box rather than a six-and-a-half-foot-tall meat wagon who would have been every human football coach's dream if he could stay in school. "Hey, Oliver," the girl said casually, continuing across the porch and down the steps.

"Hey, Autumn," Oliver replied. These were Dean's homeschool classmates.

Autumn's hair fell down her shoulders, which were barely covered by a tank top, and she wore short cutoffs and flip-flops. Oliver considered, as he often did, that Autumn would probably be pretty attractive if she wasn't a zombie. But since she was, her skin was splotchy with purple and gray decay and had rotted off in places, like almost to the bone on her left shoulder, and that just wasn't very . . . pleasant. Plus, her mother, Ariana Fitch, while apparently a great homeschool teacher, was a pretty earthy zombie and didn't believe in odor concealment. The combined scent of Autumn and her mother was practically unbearable to a sensitive vampire nose.

"Good evening, Oliver." Ms. Fitch joined them on the porch now. Her black dress was barely visible because of the hair wrapped around her. As with vampires, zombies' hair and fingernails continued to grow beyond the grave. Not only that, they grew much more rapidly than humans'. Oliver had to get his hair cut nearly every two weeks. Many zombies just chose to shave their heads or pull all their hair out, though the pulled hair usually took some of the scalp with it.

Ms. Fitch, however, hadn't cut her hair in probably thirty years. It was curled into thick blond dreadlocks and dropped like a nest of pythons off her head, wrapping completely around her waist, then around one shoulder, then the other, winding down one arm, and finally across to the other, where she held the ends in her hand.

"Hey, Oliver." Dean appeared in the doorway. "Have a good summer, guys!" he called to his schoolmates.

"Later, Aunders," Sledge called to Dean. "Let me know if you guys are going out killing or anything," he said with a smile. "I'd love that — hey, ice cream!" Sledge immediately turned and ran toward the far end of the street, as if the convenience store, which had always been there, had just appeared out of nowhere.

"'Bye, Dean," Autumn said warmly. "Maybe we can hang out sometime this summer. . . ."

"Um." Dean gulped. "Sure."

"Enjoy your vacation, Dean," said Ms. Fitch with a sly smile. She and Autumn walked around the side of the house to cut through the yards. Their pod lived beneath the nearby Safeway supermarket.

"So . . ." Oliver said. "Autumn?"

Areas of Dean's face went a slightly darker shade of purple. "Yeah, um . . . I don't know about that." He stepped back into the house. Oliver followed him through the dark living room, toward the candlelit kitchen.

"She seems nice," Oliver offered.

"I guess." Dean shrugged. "Um . . . hey, only two days until we leave!"

"Yeah." Oliver tried to sound upbeat. He was glad that Dean was coming along on the Nocturnes' vacation: That was another bonus of everyone believing Dean was his servant.

"Hey, Oliver!"

Oliver looked around Dean and felt a familiar rush of tingling nerves. There was Emalie, smiling from beside the kitchen counter. "Hey," he managed to reply.

Emalie, her hair in two braids, was busily spreading white frosting on the sides of a chocolate cake. A second spatula was applying frosting as well. It hovered in the air as if held by an invisible hand. Now it dropped to the counter and there was a rush of black, like a faint mist, across the room.

Oliver felt a slight, cool tingling by his shoulder. "Hi, Oliver," said a mousy voice.

"Hey, Jenette," Oliver said to the misty wraith. "You got away from The Shoals again?"

Jenette sighed. "Yeah, it wasn't easy, but I wanted to see you guys before you left!"

At this, Oliver's sensitive ears detected the slightest sigh from Emalie, who had finished icing the cake and was now covering it in small peanut butter cups.

"I can't believe you'll be gone for three whole weeks." Jenette slipped from one of Oliver's shoulders to the other. "I'll be so bored."

"Huh." Oliver had no idea what to say.

"You can always haunt my brother," Dean offered.

"Hey!" Dean's younger brother, Kyle, shouted from the other room.

"Oh, wait! I'll help!" Jenette called, and darted back to the counter, where Emalie had finished with the cake and was now gathering handfuls of silverware to bring to the dining room. Oliver noticed Emalie roll her eyes. Ever since Jenette had been hired by the Brotherhood to possess Emalie and slay Oliver, she had been trying to make amends by helping Emalie out. Or at least that was why she *said* she came around. . . . She always seemed pretty excited to see Oliver.

"All right, everyone, to the table!" Dean's mom, Tammy Aunders, appeared behind the kitchen counter, standing up from the oven with a tray of breaded chicken. She was improbably tall, with wild, curly hair. "Hello, Oliver," she said pleasantly, then turned her eyes to the ceiling. "Mitch!"

"Dad's still having trouble adjusting to his new night job," Dean explained as they passed through the kitchen. "He wants to be nocturnal so someone's on my schedule, or at least that's what Mom wants."

Oliver noted Tammy zipping around, doing four things at once. As usual, there were thick old library books scattered across the counter. Oliver caught a few titles: *Brains and Your Health, Preparing Raw Organ Sushi, Better Carcass Technique* . . .

They entered the dining room to find Kyle, who was eight, and Dean's sister, Elizabeth, who was ten, already seated at the table. The lights were off. Above the table, the Aunderses had replaced their light fixture with a small, candlelit chandelier.

"Hey, Oliver!" Kyle called excitedly. He was wearing a small headlamp to read a comic book in the gloom.

"Hey," said Oliver.

Elizabeth gave Oliver and Dean only a glance, then gazed sullenly back into a space somewhere in the middle of the table.

Kyle stared at Oliver as he took his seat, making Oliver squint. "I've been reading about Dracula!" he said excitedly.

"Duh, turn the light off," Dean said, and snatched the headlamp off Kyle's head.

"Eeww!" Kyle recoiled from Dean's hand. "Don't touch me!"

"Dracula, huh?" Oliver said to Kyle, trying to be polite.

"Yeah," Kyle continued, "I read he can turn into a bat, or smoke. Can you do that stuff?"

"Not yet," Oliver replied.

Kyle shrugged his eyebrows. "Oh. Well, also, I read that Dracula can control people's minds and make them into his minions. He made this one guy eat bugs!"

"I can make *you* eat bugs," Emalie said from across the table. She flashed a mischievous grin at Oliver and Dean, and then, with a nod, made Kyle's fork rise off the table. It turned and started to float across the room. "Let's go find some bugs for Kyle!"

"Stop it!" Kyle shouted, his little round face suddenly draining to white.

Oliver watched Emalie as she gazed intently after the fork. He saw her left hand gripping a small black velvet bag and knew it was one of Emalie's Orani charms. Emalie had been studying with her great-aunt Kathleen throughout the spring, learning more about her Orani powers.

Emalie was a descendant of a secret line of women. Her mom, Margaret, had been missing for two years. She had left behind notebooks full of enchantments and charms, which Kathleen had been helping Emalie decipher.

Most of what Emalie could do now involved reading people and getting inside their heads. Orani weren't big on sorcery or magic, but Emalie could manipulate simple objects by making a connection between the energy of a person's emotions and the item.

In this case, Emalie had taken Kyle's thoughts of food and bugs, combined with a bit of the fear that he secretly felt when Oliver was around, and channeled these emotions to move the fork. Oliver knew that since Kyle was young, his fears could grow quickly, and if Emalie wasn't careful, that fork really would travel all the way to the basement, spear a nice juicy spider, and bring it up to Kyle, whether Emalie wanted it to or not. This was the constant balance with the energies that Emalie could harness. If they got out of control, there could be trouble.

"Don't do that!" Kyle shouted. "Mom! The witch is making me eat bugs!"

"Kyle David!" Tammy scolded from the kitchen.

"Just kidding, Kyle," Emalie said grumpily. The fork returned to Kyle's plate with a clang.

"All right." Tammy swept to the table with two plates of chicken and macaroni and cheese. "Here you go, kids," she said as she placed them in front of Kyle and Elizabeth. She returned a moment later with a similar plate for Emalie, and one for her own seat.

"Thanks, Aunt Tammy," Emalie called brightly. Dean's mother was her dad's sister.

Now there was a shuffling and Dean's father, Mitch, trudged into the dining room, wearing a bathrobe and slippers. The little hair remaining on his head was frizzed this way and that, and his eyes were barely visible over deep bags.

"Hey, Dad," Dean said. Oliver saw Dean watching his father carefully.

"Rise and shine, Mitch," Tammy said cheerily, yet it sounded to Oliver like an order. She appeared at the table with a plate of eggs and toast and a cup of coffee.

Mitch dropped into his seat and looked around the table, seeming to glance past Dean quickly, and Oliver even more briefly. He grabbed his coffee, took a sip, then stared over his mug, his eyes finding the same lost space in the center of the table that Elizabeth was gazing into. "So," he said, "school's out for the vampires, too?" Mitch sounded very tired.

"We got out last night," Oliver replied.

"Our last day is tomorrow," Emalie added.

"Mmm." Mitch started eating his eggs.

"Oh, honey . . . Mitch is still getting used to his new hours," said Tammy as she returned to the table with one last plate. "Here you go, Dean," she added quietly.

Elizabeth glanced at Dean's plate and a thin huff escaped her scowling lips.

"Gross," Kyle confirmed.

"Thanks, Mom," Dean said unexcitedly, looking down at the heap of raw chicken carcass. "How'd it go this time?" he asked. Since Dean had returned, the Aunderses had taken to keeping chickens in a back-yard coop.

"Well, you know . . ." Tammy sighed as she headed back into the kitchen. "I did a little better with the beheading. And the defeathering is getting faster. It's no big deal." Then she added, "It's how our ancestors lived!" She almost sounded enthusiastic, but not quite.

Dean leaned toward Oliver. "She says that all the time."

Oliver nodded. He didn't envy Dean for having to eat that. Tammy's skills at preparing a carcass were definitely getting better, but the results were still rough.

Now she returned a final time, with a small juice glass of blood for Oliver. She met Oliver's eyes, but looked away quickly. "That's all I could get from the chicken." She put it down. "Sorry there isn't more. I've *got* to buckle down and get my reading done — I know I can extract blood more efficiently."

"It's plenty," Oliver said, trying to be polite.

"No, no." Tammy spun and disappeared, still talking from the kitchen. "I didn't have time to do any baking this week. . . ." Oliver was reminded of how Phlox got sometimes, when she was doing too many things at once. Tammy popped back in. "But I got you these." She placed the plate in front of Oliver and finally sat down herself.

"That's perfect," Oliver assured her, hiding his disappointment at seeing the two Twinkies on the plate. Vampires considered Twinkies practically a poisonous food, with all the junk ingredients inside them.

"Well, dig in, everyone. Here's to summer!" Tammy said with a smile, raising a glass of red wine, then glancing sideways at Oliver and Dean, as if realizing that summer wasn't something to celebrate if you were nocturnal. "Or . . ."

"No," Dean said quickly, raising his own glass of pure lemon juice (a favorite of zombies that was good for regulating bacteria), "that's cool, Mom. To summer."

Everyone toasted and then began eating. A silence fell over the table. Mitch yawned. Elizabeth ate quickly. Tammy watched everyone to make sure that they were eating and barely touched her own food. Oliver found Kyle watching him now and again. Emalie had to wait to start eating as Jenette unfolded her napkin and placed it in her lap for her.

Tammy finally took a few bites. "So," she said a moment later, "are you guys excited about your trip?"

"Yeah," Oliver replied, trying not to scowl at the taste of his Twinkie.

"I know Dean hasn't done his packing yet," Tammy said with a smile toward her son.

"Mom —" Dean sulked.

"Dean," Tammy intoned, "if you wait until the last minute, we'll end up running all over town to get things and it will be extremely stressful. What time did you say the Charion train leaves, Oliver?"

"Eleven P.M."

"Ugh," Elizabeth said softly.

"What is it, Lizzie?" Tammy asked.

Her nose wrinkled with a look like she might be sick. "I can't eat with the ... smell," she said, still staring into the table.

"Well ..." Tammy glanced guiltily at Dean, her brow furrowed. "It's not that bad, Lizzie. You can —"

"No —" Tears were welling in Elizabeth's eyes. "I can't." She sniffled.

Oliver saw Tammy's eyes momentarily well up, too. For the past four months, he'd watched the Aunders family trying to make it work with Dean. Sometimes it made Oliver feel a little jealous. Dean never had to hide who he was when he was at home. But still, both families were trying to pretend things were normal, when they just weren't. Oliver wondered if Dean's family would ever really get used to him being a zombie. Oliver had never heard of a zombie living with a human family. Could there ever be normal happy dinners, or would it always be a struggle? Would there always be tears just beneath the surface?

Of course, what they had to do at the end of dinner didn't help, either.

"It's fine, Mom," Dean said, getting up. He disappeared into the kitchen and returned wearing a large necklace of braided sage to control his smell, which, despite the sand baths and antibacterial care, could still get pretty bad in the heat.

"Is that better?" Dean asked Elizabeth.

She looked up at him with an awful, icy look, then hunched over her food without responding. Dean watched her like he was wondering if there was anything else he could say.

Forks clinked against plates as dinner continued. A loud crack sounded as Dean opened the chicken skull to get at the brains.

Kyle stood. Oliver saw that his plate was clean, and his mouth was stuffed full. "May I be excused, please?" he mumbled around his food.

"Well, honey, I—" Tammy began.

"Please, Mom? I don't want to be around for *it*."

"That's fine," said Mitch, standing as well, his plate also cleaned. "Come on, sport, let's go outside and play some games." He reached over and gave Elizabeth a silent squeeze on the shoulder before leaving the table.

Tammy's eyes wavered again as the two left.

Elizabeth had finished, too, but she remained where she was. Dean was gnawing on a leg bone, grinding it down.

Oliver met Emalie's eyes, and he gave her a nod.

"All right, well, Elizabeth, it's time," Emalie said carefully. "I'll have to get home soon."

A tear slipped down Elizabeth's cheek.

Tammy stood so quickly that she knocked over her wineglass. A puddle of crimson spread across the white tablecloth. "Come on, Lizzie," she said, a shudder in her voice. "It will be over before you know it."

She pulled up on Elizabeth's arm, but Elizabeth shook it off. She shot to her feet on her own and stormed out of the room.

"I wish there was another way," Dean muttered.

"I know," said Emalie.

They stood up and followed Tammy, and the sound of Elizabeth's angry steps, into the basement.

CHAPTER 3

Sacrifices

They descended a rickety wooden staircase into a low-ceilinged basement. Its bare concrete walls were lined with shelves of camping gear and boxes of Christmas decorations. A Ping-Pong table took up almost half the small space, a single lightbulb hanging above.

On the far side of the room, Elizabeth stood alone inside a white circle painted on the floor. Tammy stood with her feet just outside the line, reaching in and stroking Elizabeth's shoulder. Oliver and Dean joined her at the circle's edge, Jenette hovering around them, while Emalie stepped inside.

"Ready?" she asked. Elizabeth didn't reply. Her face was clenched and red as she held out her right arm and dutifully rolled up the sleeve of her sweater, exposing her bare skin up to the elbow. There, on her forearm, was a thin white scar, two inches long.

Emalie reached into her striped shoulder bag and pulled out a black film canister. She popped off the top, then glanced down to the floor. Beneath Elizabeth's outstretched arm was a thick black square of obsidian stone with a bowl-shaped depression in its center and gold hieroglyphics around its edges. This was a VanMuren's Mortar, which Oliver and Dean had obtained from Dead Désirée. In it was a small pile of soil from Dean's gravesite, a torn piece of Dean's bloodstained shirt from the night he was killed, the ash of a burned sprig of alpine spruce, and a shiny penny.

Emalie tipped the film canister, and sparkling dust of rose quartz poured into her palm. "All right." She smiled at Elizabeth. "This will be over before you know it."

"Be strong, honey," Tammy said thickly.

Elizabeth barely nodded.

Dean shifted from foot to foot.

Emalie produced a scrap of paper in her other hand and read from it: "*Enthülle den Meister . . .*" This was German, and it meant "unveil the master." Emalie breathed nervously, then said: "*Sythlysachh . . .*" She glanced at Oliver, who nodded. This word was from Skrit, and Emalie's pronunciation improved every time. It meant, "Bring forth the blood."

Demon whispers began to swirl around the room. Emalie blew the quartz powder out of her hand. The dust scattered at first, then began to gather in the air just above Elizabeth's shaking arm. It swirled and formed a narrow shape, a dagger, coming to a sharp point just above her skin. Elizabeth gasped and held her breath.

"Now," Emalie commanded.

The dust dagger slowly lowered and sliced along the white scar, reopening the wound.

"*Nnnn!*" Elizabeth cried through gritted teeth. When the cut was reopened, the dagger pulled away and scattered into a rain of dust, falling harmlessly to the floor.

Emalie reached forward, taking Elizabeth's arm and twisting it sharply.

"*Nahh!*" Elizabeth gasped.

"Careful," said Oliver quietly. Looking closely at Emalie, he saw the faintest glimmer of red in her eyes. He'd seen that before, when she entered a deep Orani state. He wasn't sure what it meant, but when it happened, Oliver felt a strong connection to her, like they bonded on some dark level. It was nice, but also dangerous for Emalie.

Drops of blood escaped the wound, running down Elizabeth's arm and falling. As the first landed in the Mortar, white smoke began to rise.

After four drops had fallen, Emalie nodded, and Tammy swooped in and snatched her daughter from the circle, immediately pressing a towel to the wound. They retreated to a nearby couch and sat, Tammy rubbing Elizabeth's shoulders as she broke down into sobs.

"It's okay, Lizzie, it's over. . . ." she soothed.

"Thanks, Liz," Dean said meekly, but neither his sister nor his mom replied.

Emalie sat down. Oliver and Dean stepped into the circle and sat with her around the Mortar. Jenette floated between Oliver and Dean. Emalie picked up a wooden spoon and mixed the contents together. Then the four joined hands.

The white smoke increased, curling upward and forming a disc above. The disc swirled around a hollow center, and in it an image appeared in white: a handprint with hollow spots on each fingertip. After a moment, the image faded and the smoke dissolved.

"All right, Dean," said Emalie, "supposedly your master's been marked again."

"A lot of good it's done us so far," Dean groaned, even as he nodded. "Thanks for doing that, though. Not that we know if it even works."

They had been performing the master location spell once a month since February. It could only be done during the waxing moon, and only lasted one lunar cycle. The spell required the blood of the direct relative nearest in age to Dean, and so each time they had to go through this torturous ordeal of drawing Elizabeth's blood. And they had to keep doing it because, so far, they had not seen anyone with that handprint "mark" that had appeared in the smoke, the mark that the library Codex had said would appear *above all conceal-ments*. They weren't even sure if the spell was working at all.

Further, Dean had yet to receive any orders from his master. It was almost as if he didn't have one, but Oliver knew that was impossible. There was a master out there somewhere.

"Well, all we can do is keep our eyes peeled," Oliver offered, "and hope we see it. Sooner or later, your master's got to at least come around to check up on you."

"Right," Dean said glumly. "*There's* something to look forward to."

Tammy and Elizabeth were moving to the stairs. Elizabeth was ranting, her words muffled by her mom's shoulder, "I don't want to do this anymore!"

Dean's face fell. "We should maybe get out of here for a while."

"I need to get home, anyway," said Emalie, wiping the red pasty residue out of the Mortar with a rag.

"Me, too," added Jenette.

They headed upstairs and cleared the dishes from the table before making their way to the door. Elizabeth and Kyle were in the living room, watching TV with Mitch.

"See ya," Dean said halfheartedly.

"Thanks for dinner, Ms. Aunders," added Emalie.

"Okay," Tammy called from the kitchen. She'd finished spraying and wiping down every surface with a bottle of bleach and was now pouring herself a large glass of red wine, her yellow rubber gloves still on.

Oliver was glad to get out in the street and to see that the sun had finally set.

"Have a good trip, you guys," said Jenette.

"Yeah," said Oliver. "See you in a couple weeks."

"I guess," Jenette moaned. "But if you need me for anything, Oliver, you can always summon me. . . . Emalie, I'll come find you the next time I can get away, okay?"

"Sure," said Emalie, not sounding very excited.

"'Kay, 'bye." Jenette slithered off into the evening gloom.

Emalie watched her go, then turned to Oliver and Dean. "Okay, I have something to tell you guys while we walk home." They zigzagged through the evening streets, still busy with humans enjoying the night. Emalie spoke slowly. "You guys know I've been working my way through my mom's old notebooks, with my great-aunt Kathleen."

"How's that been going?" Dean asked.

"Good," Emalie replied. "We've been learning all this Orani stuff, like how I moved that fork at dinner, but also, like, how to read people's thoughts and get inside their heads — don't worry," she said, "I'm not inside *your* heads."

Oliver smiled, but the idea made him nervous. If Emalie were in his head, she might notice how much he thought about, well, Emalie.

"So," Emalie continued, "we've also been trying to figure out what my mom was up to when she left. I've told you that I have dreams sometimes, where it seems like I'm with her, in her head, and we're in these old places. . . . Well, I — I'm pretty sure that when she left two years ago, she didn't mean to be gone forever."

"So what happened?" asked Dean.

"She ran into trouble," Emalie said darkly. "And now, well, she's either trapped somewhere, or maybe a prisoner, I'm not sure."

"Any idea where?" Oliver asked. He felt a flurry of excitement at the idea, glad for Emalie, and almost jealous. It reminded him of his own human parents, who might be out there somewhere. . . .

"No," Emalie continued, "but I think we figured out where she was when she disappeared. She was looking for someone named Selene. I don't really know who that is —"

"Selene?" Oliver mumbled. It sounded familiar. . . . "That's who Désirée was talking about last time we saw her."

"I don't remember that," said Dean.

"Well," Oliver continued awkwardly, "it was when she whispered in my ear."

Emalie looked over. "Dead Désirée whispered in your ear?"

"Well, sort of . . . yeah. It was weird, you know . . ."

Dean rolled his eyes. "Dude, just tell us what she said."

"Right." Oliver tried to remember the exact wording. "It was, um: *Selene is best heard through the fires that burn cold.*"

"What does that mean?" asked Dean.

Oliver shrugged. "I don't know. Except, with Désirée, it probably means, like, three things at once. But it seems like we're supposed to meet Selene, or talk to her, or something."

"I think she's in danger," added Emalie.

"Who?" Dean asked. "Your mom or Selene?"

"Well, both . . . I think my mom thought that Selene was in danger . . . and I think I know where she went to find her."

"Where?" asked Oliver.

"Italy. A town called Fortuna."

Oliver stopped. "Wait, Fortuna?" He couldn't believe the coincidence. "There's a town called Fortuna above the gates to Morosia."

Emalie nodded. "That's probably it. The town is at the base of some old volcano called Morta. In ancient mythology it was supposed to be an entrance to the Underworld."

"Morosia is built beneath Mount Morta," Oliver confirmed. "That's right where we'll be in a couple days."

"Well," said Emalie, "I'm going, too."

"No way!" Dean exclaimed. "How?"

"My dad is going to be out on the salmon boats for two weeks," Emalie explained, "so Great-Aunt Kathleen is taking me to Italy. She's calling it a cultural trip, but we're really going to look for this Selene person —"

"And your mom," Dean added, "right?"

Emalie shrugged. "I don't want to get my hopes up. . . ."

"Nice," said Dean. "This is great!" He turned to Oliver, who was busy trying to keep a calm, cool face rather than show how excited this news made him. "Do you think we'll be able to get away from your family for a bit while we're there?"

"Yeah, shouldn't be a problem," said Oliver, thinking about how things had been with his family lately. "We can meet up in Fortuna."

Emalie nodded. "Excellent."

A bright dinging sounded from up the street. "Dudes," said Dean, his voice low with reverence. "I think I hear . . ."

Oliver smiled. "The sound of Choco Tacos," he agreed with the slight upward turn of his mouth that was his biggest smile.

"You guys are dorks," Emalie chided, stepping away.

The little ice-cream truck approached, playing its tinny, happy music, and yet, was it really happy? There was something just a bit odd about the way it warbled ever so slightly off-key, like it might not be a good idea to be out alone when this ice-cream man came along.

And that was true, because as the truck pulled up, Oliver and Dean saw that the driver was Bane's friend Ty Gimble. He had his hair comically slicked back, a pointy white cap on his head, and a closed-mouth grin to hide any features that might worry the customers.

A gaggle of little kids ran ahead of Oliver and Dean. Ty grinned at the humans. "Hey there, kiddies! Who's hungry?"

Even Bane was jealous of Ty's job. Sure, Ty had to cruise the streets doling out ice cream to human kids and their annoying parents during dusk, but then, once night fell, it was almost guaranteed that he would find a child — or if he was lucky, two — still making their way home and hungry for a snack. The rectangular window of the ice-cream truck was just wide enough for Ty to pull two smaller kids through and stuff them into the freezer units before their expectant ice-cream smiles could turn into terrified screams.

Since humans weren't to be killed except on the rarest of occasions, Ty would only knock out the kids. And he wouldn't leave them in the freezers long enough to give them frostbite. It didn't take long for him to extract a pint of blood from each child, using a syringe between the toes that barely left a mark. Sometimes Ty couldn't resist taking a quick bite, but then he just used the usual vampire-bite-concealment creams and memory potions, so that afterward, the kids would find themselves back on the street corner with little idea of what had just happened, and even with a free ice cream in their strangely cold hands.

Ty's boss, Harvey, of Harvey's Discount Sanguinarium, didn't mind Ty's occasional snacking as long as he got the pints of blood to sell at his store. A few bucks from the normal ice-cream sales never hurt, either.

"Gentlemen," Ty said as happy, oblivious kids ran off with ice cream, and Oliver and Dean stepped to the window. "Where's your little human girlfriend, Nocturne?"

"Shut up, Ty," Oliver said without worry. Of Bane's friends, Ty was maybe the least evil, or maybe the most, because he truly didn't care what anyone else did with their time, or how anyone felt in general. Nothing mattered to him one way or the other, which meant that you never knew what he might do. But he probably wouldn't bother telling Bane that he'd seen Oliver. "How's business?" Oliver asked.

"Booming," Ty said with a wide smile. He banged on the freezer unit to his right, and Oliver and Dean heard a faint whimper from within. "What can I get you guys?"

"Gotta be Choco Tacos," said Dean.

"Ah, Oliver's sorry minion makes a fine choice." Ty turned around and reached down into the corner of the back freezer box, where the special Choco Tacos — the ones that had deliciously sweet possum blood added to them — were stored.

Oliver placed a few *myna* onto the counter as Ty handed over the ice cream. "Thanks, and have a lovely evening, you human-loving losers." His pleasant tone and grin never changed as he turned to an approaching group of human kids. "Who's next?"

Back on the sidewalk, Emalie emerged from the shadows. "Happy?" She was lowering her camera and slipping it back into her bag.

Oliver shrugged, loving his latest bite of chocolatey blood goodness. "Happy enough . . . Good photo?"

"Yeah." Emalie's eyes gleamed. "The light was perfect. Made the inside of the truck glow, and you guys were silhouetted . . . well, sort of. You were blurry as usual, Oliver. It was right out of a coffee-table book, except for the undead part."

Oliver chuckled around a mouthful of sweets. He liked hearing Emalie talk about her photos.

"So," mumbled Dean, his mouth also full, "how will we find you in Fortuna?"

"Right." Emalie fiddled in her bag, then pulled out a tiny object and held it out to Oliver.

"What's this?" Oliver asked as he took it. It was a small red plastic toy television, with a paper photo of Niagara Falls for a screen. There was a single yellow dial on the top. When you turned the dial, the cheap picture rolled to show a new one, also of Niagara Falls.

"I imbued it with a contact enchantment," said Emalie proudly. "When you get to Morosia, turn the dial four times forward, two back, then say my name."

"Got it." Oliver pocketed the toy.

They stopped at the next intersection. "So," Emalie said, "I guess I'll be seeing you guys in Europe."

Oliver nodded, yet with the slightest worry inside. "Be careful, Emalie."

She flashed him a brash smile. "Of course." She took off into the dark.

✸

Oliver returned home to find the downstairs quiet. The kitchen was empty, yet the plasma screen was on. It showed one of the human talk shows on a popular twenty-four-hour news channel, which was a vampire favorite for its violent war coverage. Of the three opinionated pundits who sat around a table arguing about the news of the day, the man on the right was actually a vampire named Karl Stallworth. He loved to shout about things and enrage his two cohosts. "You gotta lock these people up and throw away the key!" he was bellowing now, his jowls jiggling.

A plate of dinner waited on the kitchen island: tempura tofu marinated in shark blood. Oliver grabbed a goblet and opened the fridge. He took down a small glass bottle along with a can of Coke. He unscrewed the bottle with a hiss and poured a small amount of syrupy liquid from it: kitten blood. It was so potent, and came in such small amounts, that it had to be diluted, preferably with something sweet. Oliver popped open the soda and added it. He sat down to eat.

"Who cares how they're treated if they're evildoers?" Karl Stallworth practically screamed, his eyes just barely glowing as he watched the shock register on his cohosts' faces.

Oliver was a few bites into dinner when he heard a light clinking of glasses. Straining his ears, he caught the sound of low voices from down the hall. His mom and dad, and someone else . . . Oliver slid off his stool and started down the hall. Light spilled from the study. He heard the popping of a cork. "Blood malt?" Sebastian was asking.

"Just a nip — can't stay long." Oliver recognized the third voice. It was Tyrus McKnight, one of Sebastian's coworkers at Half-Light. Oliver could picture him, tall and gaunt, with curly hair and small round glasses, always wearing a high black turtleneck beneath his long coat. Tyrus had worked with Sebastian when they were trying to stop the Scourge of Selket, back in the winter. Oliver didn't know what Tyrus did at Half-Light, only that he wasn't an attorney like Sebastian.

Oliver concentrated on the forces and climbed up the wall to the ceiling, where he continued quietly down the hall.

There was a sound of pouring liquid.

"Thanks," said Tyrus, adding, "you should pour yourself one."

Oliver moved slowly across the ceiling to the doorway directly opposite the study, which led into the dark guest crypt. He crawled inside to the far wall and dropped to the floor, then moved along the wall until he could just see out the door and into the study.

Tyrus was sitting behind Sebastian's ancient teak desk. The glass computer monitor obscured most of his face as he flicked the mouse around. Phlox was standing over his shoulder, biting a fingernail. Sebastian wasn't in sight, which was unfortunate because of what he said next:

"So, this is the Stiletto of Alamut?"

"That's it," Tyrus replied without looking over. "I retrieved it from the ancient fortress vaults myself.

It should do the job, though I don't envy you for having to do it."

Phlox glanced toward Sebastian, deep lines of concern on her brow.

"Well, apparently, it's what needs to be done," said Sebastian darkly. There was a sound of metal against leather, as if this Stiletto was being put in its sheath.

"I still don't see why Sebastian has to be the one to do it," said Phlox, her voice edgy.

"I know," said Tyrus, "but you heard what Ravonovich said. It's a show of faith. Ravonovich thinks he has reasons to doubt."

"After all our loyalty . . ." Phlox grumbled.

"Trust me, I know," Tyrus agreed, "but you have to admit, the sign readers have been clear about what must be done if things aren't working out. Ravonovich feels that because of this whole development with the human girl, we have to take this action. . . . The prophecy must be put above any one individual, no matter how . . . important. So I'm afraid we don't have a choice."

Phlox's lips pursed. The room remained silent. Oliver felt his gut tightening into a knot.

"All right, here's the location where it must be done." Tyrus nodded at the computer screen. Phlox leaned over.

Sebastian appeared over Tyrus's other shoulder. "That's near Morosia, so the cover story will work perfectly."

"Yes," Tyrus continued. "As I've said, it's best that it's done in a remote spot, so there's no outcry from the locals. Even our kind doesn't take kindly to this type of slaying."

"And you're sure there's no other way?" Oliver could hear the worry in Phlox's voice. "Couldn't we just . . . "

"I'm sorry, Phlox," said Tyrus grimly. "I know the loss will be hard, but this is the only way. And besides, I talked to Dr. Vincent. He feels that it will be possible to make a replacement."

"I hate this," Phlox hissed.

"Phlox." Sebastian reached over and patted her shoulder. "We can do this. You know it's the right thing."

"I don't know that any of this is right anymore."

"All right, I gotta get back." Tyrus stood. "I think you have everything you need."

"I suppose I do." Sebastian nodded.

"Then I'll see you on the boat to Isla Necrata. And, Seb, hell's speed, eh?"

"I'll need it," muttered Sebastian.

Oliver sank back into the darkness, listening as Tyrus left the study and let himself out. He moved closer to the door, hearing the sound of rustling fabric, and saw his parents embracing.

"A show of faith," Phlox muttered darkly into Sebastian's broad shoulder. "Haven't we shown enough faith over all these years?" Her eyes shimmered turquoise.

"I know," Sebastian murmured. "But it will be over soon, and then we'll finally be able to get it right."

"Maybe."

Oliver slipped back to the ceiling and crept down the hall. He grabbed his dinner and headed downstairs. His thoughts were racing, spinning into tight knots of worry.

What must be done if the prophecy isn't working out . . . Dr. Vincent can make a replacement . . . We'll finally be able to get it right.

Oliver found himself shaking all over. Could they mean anything else? All the disappointment and awkward silence from his parents over the last few months . . . They didn't just think he was having problems, they thought he was a failure, not only as a son but to the entire prophecy for which he'd been created. And now what? They were going to —

It's not possible, he thought. And yet, hadn't Dr. Vincent said it himself last winter? *We can always try again. . . .*

Oliver tried to put the conversation out of his mind, and yet there was no way. It stayed with him all through the sleepless weekend to come.

CHAPTER 4

Beneath the Earth and Sea

"Oliver! Charles!"

Oliver sat in front of his coffin, the drawers beneath it open, clothes spilling out around him. Beside him, his suitcase — a sleek, black, wheeled one that his parents had picked out and, worst of all, had monogrammed with silver letters — sat empty.

"Mom! ReLAX!" Bane snapped back.

Oliver looked over his shoulder to see Bane stuffing a pile of different boots into a canvas duffel. There were his beat-up cowboy boots, a pair of cracked black railroad boots, green combat lace-ups, and even the steel-tipped pair from their family vacation to the demon rodeo in Brazil.

"What?" Bane snapped, catching Oliver's gaze. Bane had dyed the middle shock of his black hair a glow-in-the-dark shade of orange. "Trying to decide which diapers to pack?"

Oliver just huffed and turned away. He thought about pointing out how stupid it was to bring more pairs of boots on the trip than shirts, but remembered that real vampires actually thought things like boots, as well as hats and coats, were the most important pieces of clothing in terms of fashion. Vampires barely cared what shirt or pants you were wearing — they frequently wore the same ones for days — if you had a cool selection of the other items, which were all the better if they had a story behind them: the boots you took off a human victim; the hat you won from another vampire while playing cards; the jacket you stole from a needy child, and so on.

Bane stood up now and sauntered out of the room. Not accidentally, his heavy, boot-laden bag smacked the back of Oliver's head as he passed. "Don't make us late, lamb," he sneered over his shoulder.

Oliver looked back at his clothes. He had no cool coats or boots, unless you counted the few things that, like his suitcase, his parents had gotten him. Even vampires his age without demons had started their collections by now. It hadn't ever really interested Oliver. Except that he had started a different kind of collection, which he ran into now as he rummaged in his drawer. He caught a glimpse of the ivory box in which he kept a growing collection of objects from Emalie and stuffed it deep in his drawer. That was not a collection he wanted any other vampires to see. And speaking of Emalie, the reason he was gazing at his clothes right now was maybe because he was worried about which shirts and pants he should be wearing when he saw her. . . .

Just one more example, Oliver thought dejectedly, *of how I'm a failure.* Speaking of which, why worry at all about what he packed? *Since it's probably a one-way trip — no, that can't be what they meant.*

Oliver had gone over and over the conversation he'd heard the other night, but the truth was, no matter how often he tried to talk himself out of it, what else could his parents have possibly meant? Didn't their conversation mean that he'd been deemed a failure to the prophecy and now he was going to be . . . what? Slain with some Stiletto thing by his father?

He's not your real father. Oliver shook his head miserably as his mind drifted back to the winter, to Braiden Lang standing atop the Space Needle and telling Oliver that his human parents were actually alive, not killed at the hands of Phlox and Sebastian on the night they sired Oliver. It had stopped Oliver in his tracks, and he remembered the feeling he'd had afterward: He'd been excited.

But since then, Emalie had searched the newspapers for any clue to contradict the article she'd already found, the one that had clearly stated that Oliver's human parents, Howard and Lindsey Bailey, had been killed on that night sixty-four years ago. The only odd thing that Emalie had found was something she couldn't find: There was no record of where the Baileys had been buried. Oliver, Emalie, and Dean had taken a few trips to cemeteries and hadn't found them. But there were lots of cemeteries in town still to be checked.

And you may not have a chance to check them, anyway. Oliver pushed the thoughts out of his mind. He had to hang on to the thread of hope that Phlox, Sebastian, and Tyrus had been talking about something else. They wouldn't *really* slay him, would they? Even among vampires, the thought of slaying a child was almost unthinkable, no matter how disappointing the child was. . . . But then, most children weren't disappointing a prophecy that involved saving the entire vampire world. As with everything else, the rules were probably different in Oliver's case.

A low chime sounded from down the hall.

"Oliver!" Phlox's heels began tapping down the stairs.

"I'm coming!" Oliver groaned. He grabbed the clothes nearest to him, not caring what they were, stuffed them into the suitcase, and hurried out of the crypt, reaching the sewer door just ahead of Phlox.

He pulled it open to find Dean, suitcase at his side, and he was surprised to see Tammy Aunders standing nervously behind him. She seemed to have taken some time to put herself together with makeup and jewelry, yet she still looked harried.

"Hey, Oliver," said Dean.

"Hey, Dean. Hey, Mrs. Aunders, um . . ."

"My mom, uh," Dean said nervously, "wanted to say thanks to —"

"Hello, Dean." Phlox's voice was chilly behind Oliver. He saw Tammy's eyes widen, her mouth quivering slightly. Oliver turned to see Phlox, her gaze equal to the tone of her voice as she fixed a silver lizard earring with ruby eyes into her perfect white lobe.

"H-hi," Tammy stammered. Oliver could literally hear her heart pounding. "I'm Tammy Aunders."

Phlox just looked at her.

"I — I just wanted to thank you for taking my son on your vacation. My husband and I think it will be a good experience for him, considering —"

"Your son . . . ?" Phlox interrupted. Now she smiled, no warmth in her burgundy lips. "Surely you realize that *this* is a zombie. He's no more your s —"

"Mom," Oliver barked, embarrassed by her tone. "*This* is Dean's mom and she's important to him."

Phlox looked at Oliver, her expression blank, and yet, she had to obey Oliver's wishes when it came to how Dean was treated. Masters made the rules for their servants, so if Oliver said that Tammy was important, Phlox had to respect that.

"Well then, isn't it nice to meet you?" Phlox smiled wide, revealing the points of her teeth. "We're glad to have Dean along." She returned most of her attention to her earring.

Tammy looked like she might be sick, but she managed to rub Dean's matted hair with a shaking hand. "Have a good trip, Dean."

"Thanks, Mom. See ya." Dean stepped in and closed the door, then turned to Oliver. "Shall I take your bag upstairs, master?"

Oliver almost smiled, but then played along. "Oh, yeah, right. Please do."

He followed Dean upstairs, past the kitchen and into the abandoned house that concealed their underground home. Dean placed Oliver's suitcase with the other bags near the door. "I'm really glad you're coming along," Oliver said. "My family's going to make me insane, and not in the good way."

"Things haven't gotten any better with them," Dean observed.

"Worse," Oliver replied. "Come on, I'll tell you on the roof." Oliver crossed the decrepit room, passing the bathtub full of putrid water. He stepped through a large gap in the wall, where the wall looked as if it had been gnawed away by an enormous creature, exposing the rotting, splintered beams. On the other side was a sopping couch, a moldy rug, and a crumbling stone fireplace.

Oliver ducked into the fireplace and stood in the narrow space. He put his hands on the walls for guidance, felt for the forces, and began to rise up the chimney. He had just started learning to levitate at the end of the school year, but he could only do it in tight spaces like this where you only had to control the forces in a small area. Real levitation in open air would still take a while.

He rose up into the evening and pulled himself out of the chimney, then hopped down onto the sagging roof and sat among the loose shingles. Dean clambered up moments later. It was close to ten and the sun had just set beyond the Olympic Mountains. A brushstroke of pink tinged the snowcapped peaks and the edges of the wispy clouds. Below, the vibrant green was draining out of the neighborhood as shadows spread and porch lights clicked on. Oliver saw the flicker of the first bat among the branches of a tall cedar tree beside the house. It dove down into the swarm of insects around a brightening streetlight, feasting.

"Listen . . ." Oliver began once Dean was seated beside him. He recounted the conversation he'd overheard between his parents and Tyrus.

"Um, that's not good," said Dean. "So you're saying . . . you think that because you've had the problems sleeping, and at school, and now hanging out with Emalie, that your parents and Half-Light think you can't fulfill the prophecy?"

"That's what it sounded like. Like I'm screwed up, broken . . . whatever."

Oliver hoped that Dean would tell him that it sounded ridiculous, but instead he nodded. "That's possible, I guess. So what do we do?"

Oliver threw up his hands. "I don't know! What can we do? Go on vacation, wait around until my dad comes after me with this Stiletto thing. . . ."

"Well, should we run away or something? We could take off —"

"And go where?" Oliver shook his head. The thought had crossed his mind, but it didn't make sense. What would they do once they'd run?

"This may sound crazy," Dean continued, picking at a loose piece of green skin on his arm, "but did you ever think of *asking* them what's going on?"

Oliver just shrugged. The thought made him feel ill. "Why? If that really was their plan, they wouldn't tell me, would they?"

"Guess not."

"And we have to help Emalie find this Selene person."

"That will be hard if you're turned to dust."

"Yeah, well . . ." Oliver didn't know what else to say. "That's all I've got at the moment."

They turned at the sound of screeching tires and saw a taxi careening up Twilight Lane. It halted in front of the house, and the gaunt driver, Miles Frisht, stepped out, adjusting his cockeyed cowboy hat and popping the trunk. The door squealed open below and Sebastian and Bane appeared, hauling the family's bags. A moment later, Phlox rushed out with a stuffed shoulder bag, wearing a black satin dress that matched Sebastian's black suit and coat. Vampires always dressed nicely for travel. Oliver and even Bane had to wear pressed pants and their long black coats.

Sebastian dumped the bags in the trunk and checked his pocket watch. "Let's go, you two!" he called to the roof.

Oliver and Dean leaped down to the yard, then stuffed themselves into the backseat with Phlox and Bane, who turned up his nose as Dean squished in beside him.

"Man, wash your mongrel, lamb!"

"Shut up," Oliver huffed.

"Boys," Phlox hissed, finally directing some frustration at Bane. "You will behave in public."

Minutes later, they were lugging their bags down two nonworking escalators and into the grimy abandoned bus tunnel downtown. In the shadows stood four sets of gleaming gold elevator doors. Other vampires lurked about in the dank station, waiting, many dressed for work and carrying purses and briefcases.

The Nocturnes crowded into a teeming elevator. As soon as the doors slid closed, it dropped at near free-fall speed, slowed at the last second, then opened to the Charion transit hub, on the bottom floor of the underground center.

The station was alive at the start of the night, well-dressed vampires rushing about importantly toward the many entryways to Charion platforms. There were long lines at the antique ticket booths. A large display high on one wall listed the arrivals and departures in bright orange. Every minute, the letters and numbers snuffed out like fires, then relit with updated information.

Oliver stared up at the giant route map on the ceiling and felt a rush of excitement. Lines of glowing magma-light connected golden etchings that represented stations around the world. He loved the possibility of the map: all those places you could go. He traced the different routes: Seattle to Playa Del Fuego, an Underworld city beneath Los Angeles; to Naraka, the second-largest Underworld city, beneath Hong Kong; to Reykjavík, which was a popular vacation spot in the fall and winter, and on and on.

"Oliver," Dean called. Oliver saw that his family and Dean had made their way to the enormous café that dominated one whole side of the station. Its large green sign would have been familiar to any human, but not the drinks on the menu: In each case, milk had been replaced with different bloods (one notable exception was at holiday time, when vampires went crazy for egg nog). Oliver joined Dean beside a tall shelf of specially designed coffee and espresso machines that infused blood during the traditional brewing. Beside that was a display of Eternal Dark Roast coffee beans, which were blended with cayenne peppers.

Soon the Nocturnes were walking toward their train platform with foot-tall cups: Phlox with a triple-shot nonfat raptor-blend latte, Bane with a six-shot hellcat frozen drink, Oliver and Dean each with a quad mocha rouge, and Sebastian with a taller, very thin cup that held his five shots of espresso diablo.

They entered the domed tunnel to a Charion platform, feeling the rumble of arriving and departing trains in the walls and floor. The platform was crowded with other travelers. Kids scrambled about on the walls between long video screens, thin as fabric, which hung down from the ceiling and blinked with advertisements.

Soon a low, humming vibration rose up Oliver's legs all the way to his teeth, and his ears started to ache as the pressure dropped sharply. There was a rush of warm air, and everyone turned expectantly toward the clear plastic tube beside the platform.

A cylindrical Charion rocketed into the station. The moment it halted, the tube was filled with black smoke. As the train's pulsing engines cycled down to a low hum, panels of the tube slid open, and giant fans in the ceiling rumbled to life, sucking the escaping black smoke upward. The train appeared again, its silver sides charred. Large embers and chunks of molten rock tumbled off it, carving tracks through a gray film on the train's surface. The film looked like ash, but was really frost that had formed on the supercooled exterior.

The Charion doors hissed open, and passengers filed out of the low-lit interior.

"Oliver, over here," Phlox said, motioning toward the nearest doorway as if Oliver was in danger of missing the train when he was only two feet away.

"I'm right here," Oliver grumbled. This was how Phlox always got when they were traveling. She wouldn't relax until they'd arrived where they were going, whereas Oliver found the traveling the most relaxing part, especially on this trip.

The Nocturnes stepped into the train, and the echoing clatter of the platform was replaced by carpeted quiet, with the gentle stringed music of the *Melancholia* drifting through the air. They filed down the aisle, past leather seats arranged in pairs. Phlox and Sebastian took one set, Dean and Oliver the next. Bane lounged across the two behind them.

"What are these?" Dean asked. On the back of the seats in front of them were a series of brass valves. Red tubes led from these valves back up to the ceiling.

"That's dinner," Oliver replied. "There's a menu in the magazine."

The train filled quickly, crowding with families desperate to escape the sun. Oliver smiled when an old woman asked for one of Bane's free seats and he had to give it up with a sulking huff.

"Attention, please," a deep female voice intoned over the speaker system. "Charion transit line B now departing for New York City and connections to Morosia and Naraka. Welcome aboard."

The doors slid closed, and there was a sharp sucking sound that made Oliver's ears compress again.

"Ow," said Dean, wincing and holding his ears.

"The train just pressurized," explained Oliver. There was a quiet murmur of anticipation among the passengers, the volume of the *Melancholia* increased slightly, and then with no warning, the Charion rocketed forward. It rumbled, vibrating left and right, then suddenly smoothed out. "That's the magnets kicking in," Oliver added.

There were no windows on the train, but plasma panels shimmered to life on the walls. A map appeared, showing the curve of the earth, seen in a cross-section.

A dot at one end showed Seattle. There was one in the middle for New York, at the highest point of the curve, and then one on the far right for Morosia. The Charion line was drawn in yellow and looked like a very shallow U between Seattle and New York, and then again between New York and Morosia. At the lowest curve of each U, the line shaded to red.

"See where the line changes color?" Oliver pointed for Dean. "That's where the train passes through the mantle of the earth. It's cool what happens then."

It took five hours to get to New York. Oliver and Dean spent a while playing video games on screens built into the seats in front of them. The attendants passed out goblets and plates of chocolate to everyone, and they dined from the blood valves.

"They're probably not going to come around with brains, or intestine pâté, or anything. . . ." Dean mused, looking hungrily at his goblet.

"Sorry," Oliver replied.

After dinner, the Charion lights were dimmed and everyone began falling asleep. Oliver reached under his seat into his carry-on bag and pulled out his blanket, as most passengers were doing. The blanket was made of two layers of extra-fine satin mesh. The space between was filled with coffin soil. Every vampire had their own unique sleeping soil in their blanket, since vampires had different preferences for things like soil humidity and weight. Some even added bugs or worms — their crawling could create a massaging effect — but Oliver hadn't.

Sometime later, Oliver felt an elbow nudge. "Hey . . ." It was Dean. "What's happening?"

Oliver saw Dean looking around in wonder, then noticed that the walls of the Charion had changed in two ways: They were glowing a faint red, and they had become ever-so-slightly transparent.

"We're passing through the mantle," explained Oliver.

Outside the train, they could see a vague impression of swirling magma, in shades of oranges and reds. Now they passed through an area that was white hot, and the train vibrated noticeably. The walls became even more transparent, so that it looked like only a collection of seats was speeding along. Glimpses of rocks and minerals flashed by, only to be swallowed again by heat and magma.

"It's getting hot in here," said Dean worriedly. "It seems like maybe you wouldn't want the walls to get thinner when we're in the hottest places." He glanced around nervously, but most of the passengers were sleeping soundly.

"Don't worry," Oliver assured him. "We're safe. When it gets too hot, the Charion uses transdimensional magnets, and we kind of phase into a parallel world for a little while. Otherwise the train couldn't last in these conditions."

Dean didn't look totally convinced. The Charion shimmied again.

"These trains do this every day," said Oliver. "Before deep-earth travel like this, it took forever to get anywhere."

"Vampires never heard of airplanes?" commented Dean.

"Nah," Oliver replied. "For one thing, human airlines are way too unpredictable and smell terrible. There was a vampire airline for a while called Twilight Air, but they could never really figure out how to deal with the solar radiation at such high altitudes. Vampires were getting a kind of low-grade combustion fever, and every now and then a pilot would burst into flames, which was bad."

A half hour later, the sides of the train began to solidify, and the heat and red glow faded. Oliver and Dean played more video games, falling asleep on and off until the train arrived beneath New York City.

New York's Charion station was cavernous and modern, and they had to cross a sea of travelers that seemed never ending before barely reaching the train to Morosia in time. This Charion was larger, two levels, with domed windows on the top. As the train hummed out of the station, Dean looked up through the windows, seeing nothing but black.

Oliver noted his skeptical expression. "Just wait," he said.

A few minutes later, Oliver nudged Dean and pointed up. They were emerging from the ground — onto the ocean floor. Black became deep blue, with pale, harmless sun flittering through the water from far above. The train began to angle downward, nearing an almost vertical pitch, its speed increasing. Out the windows the blue-green diamond dimmed to black depths.

"Ah," Dean groaned, grabbing at his ears again.

Oliver felt it, too. "We're dropping down the continental shelf," he explained. He'd been waiting for this the whole trip. The Charion dropped like a roller coaster down the steep edge of the world, the light from the sun becoming weaker and weaker. Shadows of fish were visible for a moment, then lost in inky dark. When the black had become complete, bright white magmalights flicked on from the sides of the train, casting beams out into the darkness, catching the tiny fish, drifting debris, and the occasional glimpse of some leviathan of the deep.

Oliver watched serenely, noting that Dean was gripping the sides of his seat.

"It's almost over." Moments later, the Charion began

to level out and settled into a trench cut into the sea-floor. The lights speared upward, and Oliver reclined his seat to watch for the belly of a giant squid or sperm whale or even something stranger still.

"Dude! What was that?" Dean exclaimed, bolting up in his seat moments later.

Oliver had seen it, too. Something striding on the seafloor, stepping over their trench, its leathery belly stretching up into the dark. "We're probably passing through a borderland area," said Oliver. "It could have been anything."

Soon the blurring ocean dark had put the cabin to sleep once more.

Halfway across the Atlantic, a pleasant *ding* sounded, waking Oliver. He yawned, thinking that, all in all, he'd probably gotten more sleep on this trip than he had in the entire last weekend. With the excitement of travel, that conversation between his parents and Tyrus seemed almost unreal.

"Are we there?" Dean mumbled.

"No, but" — Oliver motioned to the windows — "check it out."

The train had risen out of the trench, and the waters around them were glowing with red light from ahead. Stretching in either direction were triangular buildings, round at the base and rising to hollow points. From their tops spouted jets of orange light and billowing clouds of ash that drifted upward into the darkness. The Charion halted, towers on either side.

"Now arriving at Atlantic One Refinery. All departing passengers report to compression chambers and prepare to disembark."

"They're magmalight refineries," said Oliver. "They're built here, where the two ocean plates are spreading apart, because magma is easy to drill for. And you need cold water and pressure for refining."

Oliver gazed off into the water, superheated around these refineries and clouded with red bacteria blooms, and wondered what it would be like to work and live here. Peaceful, he imagined.

The Charion arrived at the Morosia station several hours later. Feeling stiff and bleary they exited with the rest of the passengers and crossed the station, entering a short tunnel. It ended at a high-ceilinged cavern.

"Whoa," Dean breathed.

Before them was a wide river of black water. Torches on the wall cast no reflection on it. In fact, the river didn't really seem to be made of water. Yet there was something flowing by: a liquid concentration of energy, of force that seemed to ripple.

"That's Acheron," said Oliver. "The river of sorrow..."

"So that's, like, liquid sadness?" Dean asked.

"Technically, it's force leaving this world, but some of that energy is life, and the loss of life causes a sad feeling in humans. The river transfers energy between worlds."

As the crowd of passengers from the Charion stood at the black river's edge, a low horn sounded. As if in response, a small amber light was ignited on the far side of the river. The light bobbed in the gloom, slowly growing in size. Soon they could make out its source: a lantern hung from the railing around a large square skiff. It was a ferry, empty except for a single figure using a long pole to push it through the water.

Dean almost laughed. "You guys build trains through the mantle of the planet, and that's the best you can do for crossing this river?"

"*Tsss,*" Oliver hissed, noting a few annoyed glances in their direction. "That's New World stuff. Across this river is the Old World. You have to do things a certain way."

"You couldn't just build a bridge?"

Oliver almost smiled, but kept his voice low. "This ferry has been here since before even vampires can remember. You've always had to pay its driver to get into the true Underworld. Vampires take this kind of stuff pretty seriously."

The ferry reached the edge of the river. The driver, a tall, skeleton-thin old woman in a black gown, laid down her pole and stepped forward. One by one, the vampires approached her. She opened her large mouth, and the first passenger bowed his head and placed a *myna* coin on her tongue. She swallowed the coin and opened her mouth for the next payment. When it was the Nocturnes' turns, Sebastian handed them each a coin.

Oliver could see no eyes beneath the driver's hood. He reached gingerly into her mouth, between long, ancient brown teeth, and placed the coin, trying not to make any contact, but his finger just grazed her tongue. It was scalding hot. He had barely removed his fingers when her teeth snapped shut and she swallowed.

Dean stepped up behind him. As he reached toward the mouth, he muttered, "Wielders of chaos, guide my hand . . ." He placed the coin in and yanked his hand out.

Oliver looked at him oddly. "What are you talking about?" he asked.

"Huh?" Dean asked. "Oh, nothing. Just nervous."

The vampires stood silent as the ferry slowly crossed the black river. The only sounds were the regular plunks of the driver's pole and the faint gurgle of the water. Oliver found himself wondering where Acheron began, and where it ended. He'd never thought about that before, and never heard anyone talk about it. Like the ferry, the river just *was*.

Oliver wondered why he'd even had the thought. Maybe it was because of his brief moment in The Shoals back in February, when Jenette had hid him from the Brotherhood. (The Shoals were areas on the edges of the worlds, where spirits like wraiths lived.) Or maybe it was because of their time in The Yomi, the underground market that was built on a border between many worlds.

After being in such places, Oliver had found himself considering how things were connected, how the realities seemed to flow through one another and how, even though a vampire could sense these things so much better than a human, there still seemed to be some larger purpose to it all that he couldn't quite see.

The ferry reached the far side. Everyone disembarked and passed under a large archway carved into the cavern wall. Enormous Corinthian columns towered on either side. A hall lined with torches sloped steadily downward. Vampires always preferred it very warm, and down here it was not only warm but also sticky, almost tropical.

"Where's the magmalight?" Dean asked, squinting in the flickering gloom.

"They don't use it in the Old World. It's too modern."

The tunnel ended on a wide terrace, at the top of a grand staircase. Below, in a cavern beyond measure, stood the ancient Underworld city of Morosia.

CHAPTER 5

Old vs. New

It was a world of red light and stone. Oliver's eye was immediately drawn to Phlegethon, the molten river of magma flowing through the center of the city, crossed by black iron bridges. On either side of the canal loomed enormous stone buildings: There were temples, spires and towers, all intricately lit by torches, and in the exact center, largest of all, a colossal Mayan pyramid, with a black cauldron of fire burning at its peak. It looked as if someone had been collecting signature buildings from the great civilizations of human history, and that was somewhat true, as Morosia had existed through all of ancient times.

"Kinda looks like Las Vegas," Dean remarked.

Cobblestone streets led away from the giant structures along the river, back into a twisting labyrinth of low buildings. The cavern walls were covered with apartment buildings, in the style of ancient pueblos, which rose to dizzying heights in the murky, smoky dark.

"Can we go downtown first?" Bane asked, sounding as genuinely excited as he ever had.

"We're expected right away for dinner," said Phlox. Since about New York, her mouth had taken on a permanent tight frown, and her scent was tense. She started quickly down the wide, angling stairs to the left. "Our train was a little late, so keep up!"

They weaved through the narrow streets, passing shops and open-air markets, and there was a general din and stench to the place that Oliver found overwhelming, but maybe a little intriguing. Even he had to admit that the Underworld had a relaxing air of simplicity and darkness.

Reaching the pueblo walls, the Nocturnes lined up for one of the manual elevators, which ran up the outside on thick ropes and pulleys. It was operated by two zombies in nondescript gray clothes.

"I'm not going to have to wear that, am I?" Dean asked, gazing dejectedly at the zombies.

"Only if I make you," Oliver replied.

"Ha ha."

They rode the squealing contraption up thirty floors, then stepped off onto a narrow rock walkway. Squeezing their way along, they ducked into a cramped alley, and Phlox stopped in front of an apartment door. Oliver watched her take a deep breath, then knock. There was a muffled exchange of voices from inside. The door

< 77 >

creaked open. A burst of spices greeted Oliver's nostrils: cinnamon, cloves . . .

"Well, they arrive at last!" a thin voice hissed, and Phlox's mother, Myrandah, appeared. She was in her early four hundreds and still stood fairly straight despite her age. She had most of her skin, and her teeth were as white as ever behind black-painted lips. As she stepped out of the dim apartment, the layers of beads and crystal jewelry that she couldn't get enough of jangled on her wrists and around her neck. She wore a long black dress that flowed to the ground, with a high, embroidered collar that mingled with the many carved earrings that hung low from her ears. Her hair was platinum like Phlox's, yet pulled back and piled in thick curls atop her head.

The combination of the dress and the hair was so similar to Phlox that Oliver noticed his mother reach up and quickly stroke at her own hair. He wondered if she was trying to make it look neat, or was worried because it wasn't as ornately done, or was checking to make sure it didn't look just like her mother's. Oliver guessed that it was a bit of all three.

"Hello, Mom," Phlox said, and leaned in as Myrandah offered a cheek.

"Hello, my darling Phloxiana. And where are the precious hellspawn?" she asked affectionately, darting right past Phlox and seizing Bane and Oliver in a single hug.

She pulled back and smiled warmly at the two of them. "Look at the darling young . . ." Her eyes momentarily glowed pink with emotion. Then she glanced past Oliver and spied Dean. Her lips tightened to a knowing grin. "Ahh, yes . . . Oliver brings along his pet. What did you name it?"

"He's Dean," Oliver answered awkwardly.

Myrandah reached out and stroked Dean's shoulder. "Does it obey its master?" she asked.

"Yeah —" Oliver stammered. "But he's my friend, too."

"Ha! Of course it is! A vampire's best friend." Myrandah turned to Bane. "And ah, yes, how fine and lethal this one becomes. . . ." Her eyes glowed as she rubbed Bane's arm, but Oliver noticed her cast a lightning-fast glance at Sebastian that didn't seem as pleasant. "I bet he excites at the notion of a real blood hunt with the cousins for once."

"Definitely," Bane sneered excitedly.

"Mother," Phlox groaned, "Charles doesn't need to spend his whole time —"

"*Tsss!*" Myrandah interrupted. "What else are the young adults like *Bane* supposed to do?" she countered, making sure to use Bane's chosen name. Oliver could imagine how much Bane had just enjoyed that. Myrandah turned, still smiling, and immediately reached up and grasped one of Phlox's earrings: the tiny silver lizard head with ruby eyes. "Why, how Phloxiana favors the *modern* things," she commented.

Oliver watched Phlox's mouth tighten as she fought a reply.

And as if to finish her act with a flair, Myrandah glanced casually over Phlox's shoulder to Sebastian, and her eyes narrowed slightly. "Oh . . . and she brings the husband along. Aren't we lucky?" Then she spun and started inside. "Enter!" she commanded.

Phlox and Sebastian trudged silently after her.

"Grandma's awesome." Bane chuckled.

The cluttered apartment was lit by long rows of candles mounted on the walls. A short hall led them into a main room, where a long dining table took up almost the entire space. There was no kitchen to speak of, only a brick oven on the far wall, and no appliances like refrigerators or stoves. The walls displayed helmets, weapons, and other more gruesome trophies from human victims, or the wars and revolutions that vampires had a hand in causing.

"They've arrived at last, have they?" a raspy voice hissed. It was Phlox's father, Dominus, looking up from his hunched position at the table.

"Dad, the train was barely late," Phlox huffed.

Three other chairs at the table were already filled, by Phlox's brother, Ember, and Oliver and Bane's cousins, Misère and Gustav. Their mother, Sylvana, had been slain a decade ago. Ember was older than Phlox, with thinning hair and a weathered face. He wore a rumpled blue coat, an officer's jacket from the Napoleonic Wars, its condition noticeably threadbare compared to anything Phlox and Sebastian would wear.

As everyone took their seats, there was a knock at the door. Myrandah hurried over. A young man stood outside, holding a long, thin, black glass bottle with a bulbed base in one hand and a tiny iron pitcher in the other. Each was stopped with a cork. Myrandah exchanged *myna* for the bottles and brought them straight to the table. She placed the small pitcher in front of Oliver. "Grandma remembers how he favors the tiger's blood," she cooed.

"Thanks," Oliver replied.

"And this," she said, "for the rest, fresh from the local oubliette." She held up the bottle. "A few *myna* more for the torture-draining, but how worth it!"

"The very best." Dominus nodded.

Everyone had only a goblet in front of them. As the bottle of human blood was passed around, Myrandah delivered a plate to Oliver that held a dish called vesselage. It was a spongy white cake with a latticework of thin red candy tubes spiderwebbing through the cake. Lying on the plate, spiced blood seeped from it in a pleasing way.

"It's great, Grandma," Oliver commented after a bite.

"Suck up," Bane sneered, and Misère and Gustav nodded in agreement. Misère was a short girl with a round face, her mouth down-turned in a perpetual pout. Her black hair had shocks of gold, and was pulled back and spun around two ivory sticks. She had powdered her face a pure white and painted her lips with shimmering gold as well. She wore a red silk cheongsam, embroidered with gold and fixed by a line of buttons down her right side. Gustav had long brown sideburns and wore a black pinstripe suit with a frilled collar and a tie.

Sitting there beside them, Bane should have looked like the dangerous one, slouching carelessly, with his wild hair and black T-shirt from the band the Petrified Hearts, which displayed an image of open ribs and a stone heart within. And yet he looked somehow very tame compared to his cousins. They sat perfectly straight, faces blank, and there was something calm and lethal about them: a sense that they knew many things you didn't.

"Yes, the taste of charcoaled sugar," Myrandah explained, as she did every visit. "Aged in deep caverns as only the Underworld can provide. What a treat it must be for Oliver."

"Yes, we've heard," Phlox said tightly.

Everyone tended to their goblets. The grandparents

asked about Oliver's schooling. The cousins joked with Bane about how little killing he'd done.

"Just take me out there," Bane said eagerly, "and I'll make up for my sheltered upbringing."

"*Neelesthth*," Dominus agreed in Skrit.

"So, Sebastian . . ." It was Uncle Ember. Oliver looked up, realizing that this was the first time anyone had really talked to Sebastian. "Why don't you tell us about your all-important work at . . ." He paused and his voice went slightly sour, as if his next words were distasteful: "Half-Light?"

Silence fell over the table.

Sebastian glanced briefly at Ember, then took a slow sip from his goblet. "Things are fine," he replied. "We've had a good few years. . . ."

Myrandah sniffed with disdain.

Oliver watched as his father paused and looked around, calmly taking in Ember's glare and the others' disapproving gazes. Oliver was surprised that things were getting so tense, so fast. It was almost as if the family had been waiting to pounce on Sebastian. Oliver knew that the Old World vampires disapproved of all the modern ways in the New World — of the medical sciences and philosophy that the New World vampires embraced. Even the idea that you could feed on humans without killing them was offensive in the Old World.

But this reaction seemed more intense than their last visit, although that had been a while ago.

"Now I know," Sebastian continued, sounding almost defensive, which Oliver couldn't remember hearing before, "that the Consortium doesn't have the best reputation in these parts, but it's important work that we do."

Oliver tried to take a quiet bite of cake, but his fork clanged on the plate. Dominus slurped his blood.

"Not everyone shares that opinion." Ember's eyes had started to smolder jade green.

Sebastian nodded slowly. Phlox reached over and rubbed his arm as he continued: "Look, Ember, I'm well aware that some of you —"

"Well that's the problem right there, isn't it?" Ember snapped, looking up and down the table for support. "He refers to us as *you*. We're all vampires, Sebastian, but you New Worlders seem to consider yourselves superior."

"Hold on, Ember . . ." Phlox countered.

"No, it's fine," Sebastian said calmly, yet his eyes were glowing as well. "Your brother obviously feels that this needs to be said in front of everyone, and before we've even had a chance to settle in. Let him finish his thought."

"Listen to that high and mighty tone," Ember scoffed. "Vampires have lived a certain way for centuries.

Then you come along with your theories and your abominations —"

Oliver felt Myrandah's eyes on him.

"You might want to be careful, brother-in-law," Sebastian warned.

"But you're the ones who should be more careful, don't you think?" Ember was almost shouting now. "You question things that ought not be questioned." Ember glanced at Oliver. "Prophecies are meant to be fulfilled in their own time. It is not the way to *create* an answer."

Dominus hissed in approval. It was clear what Ember meant: Oliver had been created to fulfill the prophecy. Was he the *abomination* that Ember was referring to? It sounded like it . . .

Ember continued, "And how do you even know you're reading the prophecy correctly? Our scholars find no such simple answer in its meaning! And yet Half-Light foolishly rushes ahead, ignorant of the dangers —"

"That's enough!" Phlox slammed her goblet onto the table. "It's always the same with all of you. How can you deny the yearning of the true *vampyr*? How can you not want freedom from this world, this prison?"

"PRISON!?" Myrandah suddenly roared. Her eyes burned, and her voice thinned to a sinister hiss. "You are fools to seek freedom from this world. Earth is death's paradise! A bounty made of flesh and chaos!

Could the twisted world of humanity be any more perfect for vampires?"

"Perfect?" Phlox countered. "You call being trapped in a human body, having to feed on lowly mortal creatures while living in that fear of being turned to dust, a paradise? Why can't you see that the *vampyr* within us yearns for true freedom! To return to the higher dimensions we were banished from, to live as spirit energy, immortal, fearless! How can you not feel it crying out inside you?"

"Bah!" Myrandah snapped, waving her hand at Phlox and Sebastian. "The tongues on these young to speak of the *vampyr* like it is a dirty human. To say that it yearns and cries . . . It only craves! And earth provides!" She thrust herself out of her chair and stormed from the room.

"See Grandma's claws," Misère said, her mouth registering the slightest smile, which made her seem all the more satisfied. Beside her, Bane wasn't laughing.

Oliver sat frozen.

"This would be a good time for me to leave," said Sebastian tersely. "Thank your wife for dinner," he said to Dominus, then pushed back from the table and swept out the door.

Phlox turned viciously to her brother. "Happy?"

"Are you, Phloxiana?" Ember countered.

Dinner passed in silence, though there was no silence in Oliver's head. His relatives thought he was an abomination. . . . That was a new low. And they not only thought that Half-Light was wrong to try to fulfill the prophecy by making Oliver, it sounded like they also thought Half-Light might be reading the prophecy wrong. *I've got to hear that prophecy for myself some-day*, Oliver thought.

He wondered if this new, urgent anger in his relatives was because Oliver was getting older — if having a demon dream was any indication — and that the time to fulfill the prophecy was getting closer. *So maybe they'll be glad to know that your parents are going to sacrifice you and start again.* His parents definitely sounded defiant during the argument. They believed in the prophecy, in opening the Gate. It seemed like just more evidence that they would do whatever it took to fulfill it . . . *like not letting their failure of a son get in the way*, Oliver thought darkly.

Either way, dinner left Oliver with a sinking feeling. Not only was he a failure to the prophecy in the New World, he was apparently also a failure for being the child of the prophecy in the first place. Were there any more ways, he wondered defeatedly, that he could fail?

CHAPTER 6

Seventh Moon

"These are the least *modern* earrings I have!" Oliver heard Phlox shouting as he passed his parents' room early the next evening. He heard Sebastian, who hadn't returned home until sometime after Oliver had gone to bed, grunt in agreement.

Oliver was sharing the other guest room with Bane, who had already left for the night with the cousins. They were headed to the surface to raid a human village with some of the other teens and likely bring their victims back to the oubliettes, which were special torture dungeons.

Dean was in their room, rubbing a salt balm on his face to keep his mold under control. He was sitting on the edge of the guest coffin, which was a simple open pit of soil that Oliver and Bane had to share. Dean was hunching over a tiny hand mirror that he held between his knees, as there were no mirrors in a vampire home.

"So, how was it up there?" Oliver asked. As a zombie, Dean had to sleep on the pueblo roof.

"Dude, pretty cool, actually," said Dean cheerily. "There's, like, fifty other zombies up there. They had a bonfire going with a big roast of all these different animal heads and stuff. They're not so fun to talk to, but the brains were good, and after eating, they all slept like, well, like the dead."

"Sounds kinda fun," Oliver said, partly imagining the idea of actually sleeping well.

The door popped open and Phlox stuck her head in. "Oliver, your grandmother wants to take you down to Tartarus now. So let's go."

After discovering that in his haste to pack he hadn't brought any other pairs of socks, Oliver and Dean found Myrandah in the kitchen. Phlox was trying to help her get her coat on.

"*Tsss*," Myrandah hissed.

"Mother, if you'd just let me hold the other sleeve —"

"How Phloxiana tries to help *now*," Myrandah huffed, "when Myrandah is left with only her own help in the five years between visits."

Phlox bit her lip and dropped the sleeve. "All right, then."

Oliver looked around. "Where's Dad?"

"He had more business to attend to," Phlox muttered, sounding envious.

"Quickly!" Myrandah barked from the door. "The fates pay best before midnight."

"What's she talking about?" asked Dean.

"You'll see," Oliver replied.

Below the pueblos, they weaved through the narrow cobblestone streets. Many of the shops were vacant, their entryways boarded up. There were few vampires moving about this early in the evening, and none were as well-dressed as the vampires Oliver usually saw in Seattle.

"Look around you, Oliver," Myrandah grumbled. "A once grand city, its splendor fallen. *Tsss* . . . This was the model of ancient civilizations! From Morosia and Naraka, the vampires ruled every shadow of the earth. Living in splendor, starting wars, causing chaos, and feeding on the flesh as we pleased!" As Myrandah walked, her hunch took on a bounce with her step, as if she was a large lizard. "And what now? To the surface they go, choosing an existence like the vermin, like the humans! To dodge the sunlight in order to pursue their twisted '*modern*' life."

"You've already made it clear how you feel," Phlox muttered halfheartedly, like she knew it would do no good. "Do I have to remind you that our '*modern*' ways are the reason you have true grandchildren?"

"And they are special," Myrandah said with sudden tenderness. "It is nice to have these little ones to nurture and raise. The teens are so independent right from the start. How proud we are when they are off to wild, yet how we still long to nurture them." She stopped and ruffled Oliver's hair just like Phlox did . . . or used to. She hadn't done that in months. Myrandah went on: "But then to see them so infrequently . . . for what good reason?"

Phlox shook her head like she was exhausted. "Why bother trying to explain it to you?"

"Because Phloxiana knows her word-serpents are folly," Myrandah spat. "Look at Oliver, a good inch taller than the last time I saw him, and with the weight of the world on his shoulders —"

"All right, that's enough," Phlox snapped.

"And what about Bane? Dear Bane, who still endures echoes of all that pain, without the power of his elders to support him —"

"What pain?" Oliver asked immediately.

"Mother, I said *enough*!" Phlox's eyes flared turquoise. "I think you've made your point and then some."

Myrandah looked at Phlox with narrowed eyes, then glanced at Oliver. "Have I?" She turned and trudged ahead. Phlox followed after her.

"Whoa," Dean mumbled beside Oliver. "Having a good time, huh?"

Oliver nodded. Clearly, once again, Myrandah had said things that related to Oliver. It occurred to him that Myrandah might be one member of his family who'd be willing to explain some things to him, if he could find the right moment . . .

They reached a black iron bridge. On the other side was the massive Mayan pyramid with its cauldron burning at the top, as if the building itself were a smoldering volcano. This was Tartarus. The monolithic building shimmered in the heat rising off the magma river.

"This place is, um, large," commented Dean.

"It's the center of Underworld life," said Oliver.

Gusts of hot air blew over them as they crested the bridge. Here there were crowds, and Oliver saw many sharply dressed, tall-standing New World visitors being led around by their stooped Old World relatives. Below, the magma of the river Phlegethon streamed through the canal, glowing orange. Chunks of black crust floated on the surface, cracking apart and re-forming. They passed a child who stood with her back to the canal and threw a *myna* coin over her shoulder. It hit the magma and melted with a hissing jet of flame.

"It's good luck," Oliver explained to Dean. "It's like when a human throws a coin in a fountain, only better: That wish just sits there on the bottom of the water until it's taken by someone cleaning up or whatever."

They passed through impossibly tall metal doors and entered Tartarus. Myrandah and Phlox were heading straight into the chaos in front of them, but Dean pulled Oliver to a stop.

"Um," Dean called over the incredible noise, "I thought you said this was the center of Underworld life."

"Right."

"So then why does it look like a giant casino?"

"Because it is," Oliver answered. Before them stretched an endless floor of slot machines and gaming tables, lined with restaurants, entertainment stages, and fighting cages. Above, more floors of gaming reached the ceiling, which was open at its peak. The round base of the giant cauldron hung over the space. Thousands of vampires caroused about, shouting and hissing to one another over the near-constant din of bells, game music, and clinking coins. Thick clouds of cigarette smoke hung throughout the room.

"There," Oliver said, pointing to where Myrandah was hunching down in front of a machine. They made their way over and found her staring blankly at a poker game as if she were in a trance. This machine, like all those in Tartarus, ran on gears and pulleys. The screen was simply a glass pane with the cards flipping on wheels behind it.

With one hand, Myrandah whipped across a line of levers as she chose cards to keep or discard. Pulling a lever made one of the card wheels spin. Her other hand shot in and out of a black leather purse and dropped *myna* coins into a slot.

"I'm going to the bar!" Phlox called over the din.

"Mom, can Dean and I head off on our own?" Oliver asked.

"Spend some time with your grandmother first," Phlox said with a dismissive wave of her hand, and shot off toward the safety of the bar and a crystal goblet.

Oliver frowned. "How's it going, Grandma?" he asked.

"Three queens' blood!" she shouted as a three of a kind, queens, appeared. "Fortune smiles." Her gaze stayed on the game. One hand flicked over the levers. The other hand pumped in coins.

Oliver waited another minute, wondering if this was a good time to ask Myrandah about her many veiled comments.

"Curse you, traitor jack!" she shouted at a jack of spades that had appeared on the screen to ruin her flush of hearts.

Maybe not. Oliver turned to Dean. "Let's get out of here."

"Fine by me," Dean replied. He turned — and slammed right into a stooped old vampire hobbling by. A heavy black bag of *myna* sailed out of the man's hand, slapping to the floor. Coins spilled everywhere —

"*Tsss!*" the room seemed to hiss in chorus. Every single vampire within sight froze still. All eyes fixated on the slur of shiny coins scattered across the red carpet. A quiet, whispering sound crept from every mouth.

"What's going on?" Dean asked.

Oliver was stuck staring at the floor as well. It was all he could do to reply: "Eighty-one — eighty-two — we have to count," he managed, ". . . eighty-nine — ninety — ninety-one . . ." He had no choice: His brain was completely consumed and he was powerless to fight it. Vampires were unfortunately obsessed with counting. It was something Oliver's brain was doing all the time without him ever thinking of it, and it was part of the reason why Phlox kept such an organized kitchen. Faced with a set of disorganized objects, especially scattered like these coins, a vampire had to count them. It had been a weakness throughout history. At least this wasn't a handful of rice or poppy seeds. Oliver was actually a fairly fast counter by vampire standards, which meant he was fast to the point of disbelief in human terms.

"Dude, you're kidding," said Dean.

"Nope . . . one hundred sixty-three — four — five — six — seven . . ."

Moments later, vampires around the area began sighing with relief, breaking from their paralyzed poses and moving on, having successfully counted the coins.

"Three hundred forty-eight," Oliver announced with similar relief, rolling his shoulders.

Soon all the vampires had finished, and when the old man whose coins were on the floor saw the last vampire nod and walk away, he bent down to pick them up.

"So it's a thing with all vampires?" said Dean as he and Oliver moved into the crowd.

"Yeah," Oliver replied. "We're doing it all the time."

Dean glanced around. "So, like, what are you counting?"

Oliver shrugged. "Ask me."

"How many slot machines in that row right there?"

"Eighty-six," Oliver answered immediately. He didn't even realize that he'd been counting until he thought about it, and then the information was already there, counted and sorted. "Forty-three poker machines, eighteen nickel slots, nine —"

"Okay, I get it already. You're making my head hurt just talking about it."

They walked on through the massive room, passing a large iron cage hanging from the ceiling, its walls lined with racks of weapons. By the door were two helmets made of metal, with open holes for faces, but then thick collars that would protect the neck for later feeding. "For humans?" Dean asked.

"Yup," Oliver replied.

Now they passed a large lounge area with wide leather couches facing a wall of televisions. These TVs were the only modern technology within Tartarus, and they flashed with news footage of wars, elections, famines, floods, droughts, disease outbreaks, and, curiously, the English sport of cricket. To the right of the televisions was an electronic board listing the various bets: the odds of a war breaking out or ending, the over-under on people being displaced by a flood, and the point spread on the current cricket match.

They reached a large area in the center of the building that was laid out with gaming tables.

"How m —" Dean began.

"Fifty-four," Oliver said. "Twenty poker, twenty-two blackjack —"

"Dude . . ." Dean shook his head. "How do you have time to think?"

"It's just how we're wired," said Oliver. "It's why we like these games so much. Here, let's play for a sec." Oliver had gotten a glimpse of a roulette table they were passing. They didn't really have time to play, but Oliver couldn't resist. He sat on a stool at the end of a long green felt table with wooden sides.

"Shouldn't we get to Emalie?" Dean asked.

"Yeah, but . . ." Oliver could feel his brain relaxing as he surveyed the numbers. They were soothing. What appeared to be random in a game like roulette was often of mystical significance, not that a human would ever be able to tell. They just thought it was about money. And it was about money, but it was also about connections and fate, like a tiny version of how the worlds and forces worked.

At the far end was a double roulette wheel, one circle of black and red numbers spinning above the other. Human roulette had only thirty-six numbers, but this green felt was covered with sixty-four numbers in a four-by-sixteen grid. Eight was an important number to vampires. It represented both good fortune and sacrifice, which made it a key number in many of the gambling games in Tartarus. Vampires on all sides were reaching out and either laying chips carefully onto the numbers or onto the lines and corners between them.

The chips were also different than what humans used. . . .

"Are those teeth?" Dean asked.

"Yeah."

"Human?"

"Nah," Oliver replied. "They're goat. Human teeth are only used on the real high-roller tables." He produced a small stack of *myna* from his pocket and placed them on the felt.

The croupier, a tall, severe-looking vampire in a white tuxedo who ran the table, noticed Oliver's money and, using a short white stick with a black hawk's talon at the end, slid the *myna* away. He busied about, and then used the talon stick to push back a brass ring holding a meager number of teeth, each of which had a hole drilled through it.

Oliver slid three teeth from the ring and placed them on the table.

"Minimum bet is five," said the croupier in his low, vibrating voice. Oliver frowned and added two more. He only had ten.

"This will be quick," he muttered to Dean. He looked out across the sea of numbers, jeweled hands flicking about, placing chips here and there — to find a face staring at him. A vampire girl, about his age, with pale lavender eyes, standing beyond the wheel. Her face was half in shade beneath the hood of a blue velvet cloak. Her straight, magenta hair just peeked out around her neck. Oliver had a surprising thought: *beautiful*. He looked away as fast as he possibly could.

"No more bets," the croupier announced.

Every vampire at the table began lip clicking, staring at the table. "Seventy-one," Oliver said with relief a moment later. That was the number of chips in play on the table. The rest of the vampires were relieved to have this number noted as well.

The croupier's hand flicked out and tossed a small white ball into the top wheel. It spun, then began to bounce among the numbers. Everyone watched, transfixed.

The ball danced around, then fell through a hole onto the lower wheel, to gasps of disappointment and delight. With a last high bounce, it settled in a number.

"Twenty-eight," said the croupier. Many vampires hissed angrily.

Dean slapped his shoulder. "Dude!" Oliver had won on the date of his birthday. The croupier was steadily putting sixty-three teeth on a ring, which he then slid to Oliver with his white wand.

"Wow," Oliver mumbled. He was surprised, excited, and yet distracted: There seemed to be a strong scent of lilacs in the air, overwhelming the pungent cigarette smoke . . . and there was something dizzying about that scent —

"You're good at the numbers." Oliver froze. It was a girl's voice: *the* girl. She had leaned in right beside him, elbows on the table, staring straight ahead at the numbers. "It's exciting, isn't it?"

Oliver struggled to make words come out as sounds. . . .

"*I* think so," the girl said, answering her own question.

"Yeah," Dean agreed as Oliver continued to malfunction. "Look at that pile of teeth."

The girl turned and aimed a cold, bothered look at Dean. "That's not what I meant." She turned to Oliver. "Lythia," she said simply.

Oliver felt like he'd been speared by her lavender eyes. He finally looked down to see her hand extended toward him. "Um, y-you?"

"Yes, that's my name."

"He has a name, too," said Dean, nudging Oliver in the back.

"Right, I'm Oliver. This is Dean."

Lythia turned to the table. "Will you play again?" Her eyes lit up at the thought.

What was she talking about? *The game.* "Oh, right," said Oliver, noticing that everyone at the table was laying chips again. Oliver grabbed five teeth, then another ten so he would look daring, and started spreading them around.

"Can I pick a number?" Lythia asked. Again, her lavender eyes focused right on Oliver and he found himself feeling curiously broken.

"Sure," he managed to reply. Lythia reached over and plucked a tooth from his ring. She held it close to her face, gazing at it quizzically. "What do you see, little minion of fate?" Then she cocked her head, like she was listening carefully to the tooth's answer.

Oliver felt Dean leaning by his other ear. "Um . . ."

"Really?" Lythia replied to the tooth. "Well, you *do* know best, don't you?" She stretched far out over the table and placed the tooth on 7. As she did, her shoulder brushed across Oliver's. The smell of lilacs increased.

He felt something close to nauseous, if feeling nauseous could be a good thing. Why was she having this effect on him? And then Oliver recognized the *presence* that this girl had. Lythia may have looked just about his age, but she had a demon.

"No more bets," growled the croupier. He spun the ball around the top wheel.

Lythia stared fervently at the ball and mumbled quietly to herself: "Wielders of chaos, guide my hand . . ." The ball clattered against the spinning numbers, staying on the top wheel and settling on:

"Seven," announced the croupier.

Oliver turned to Lythia. She smiled knowingly. "Now that's just about perfect, wouldn't you say?"

"I — I would," said Oliver. "You won."

Lythia rolled her eyes. "Well, yeah, there's that, but I won on *seven*. You know, 'cause of seventh moon."

Oliver didn't know what she was talking about, or maybe he did. If only his brain would work! "Seventh moon?" he asked.

"Of course." Lythia reached over and gave his shoulder a playful tap. "Some think it's a silly Old World custom. I think the seventh moon rising really does have power. And it's the biggest night for mystical sacrifice."

Oliver felt a flash of worry. *Sacrifice?* Little that happened these days seemed to be coincidence. After what he'd heard his parents and Tyrus say . . . "So, when is seventh moon?" he asked.

"Tomorrow night," Lythia replied, her voice lowering in wonder. "And you never know what it will mean. I'm sure you've heard the rumor that something big is happening this year." As she spoke, she calmly wrapped her hands around all the winning teeth that had just arrived in front of Oliver and slid them over as her own. "After all, it's common knowledge that more oracles are imbued with prophecy on seventh moon than on all other risings combined. Like Selene."

Oliver started. "Did you say Selene?"

"I did." Lythia reached out to place teeth, brushing him again.

Oliver scrambled to keep his balance — and his cool — and to understand what he was hearing. "You mean Selene is an oracle?"

"No more bets," the croupier announced, and sent the ball spinning.

Lythia glanced at Oliver with a pitying smile. "Oliver . . . *an* oracle? That's a little insulting, isn't it? After all, she's the oracle who gave the prophecy of the Nexia Gate. It's, like, the most popular prophecy in the New World. You know the *prophecy,* don't you? Every kid does. About a boy who will —"

"Right," Dean began when he saw that Oliver was stuck in his tracks again, "the one about a kid who could open the Nexia Gate and free the vampires from Earth."

"See?" said Lythia, smiling coyly. "Even your minion knows."

"I — I just forgot for a sec," Oliver stammered. Lythia's smile grew and, with it, Oliver's flush of worry. She was looking at him almost like she *knew* the prophecy was about him.

"Seven," the croupier reported mournfully.

Oliver turned to the table and watched as all the teeth he'd laid on other numbers were raked away, and another ring of winnings was pushed toward them and grabbed by Lythia. "You don't mind, do you?"

"Er . . ." Oliver began.

"He doesn't mind," said Dean.

Lythia stood straight and sighed, satisfied, her finger flicking over the pile of teeth. "Seventh moon," she said pleasantly. "I was lucky to meet you, Oliver . . . ?"

"Nocturne," Oliver added like a good student. "And you're Lythia . . . ?"

"I am." She kept gazing at Oliver. "Thanks for the help," she said, returning a single tooth to him to replace the one she'd borrowed. She gathered the other two rings of teeth in her hands. "Maybe I'll see you around again?" she asked.

"I —"

"You will," Lythia answered for him. She backed away from the table and was instantly swallowed by the crowd. Oliver looked down at his chips, at once relieved and disturbed.

Dean patted Oliver's shoulder. "Come on, killer, let's go meet up with Emalie."

CHAPTER 7

The Search for Selene

"**Y**ou were pitiful," chided Dean as they climbed the wide staircase out of Morosia.

"I wasn't —"

"*Pitiful*. It was hilarious."

Oliver rolled his eyes. "Whatever. Who cares? We need to find this Selene." Oliver's thoughts whirled. Selene was the oracle who had predicted his destiny. *That's why Désirée mentioned her.* Oliver remembered asking Désirée if she knew anything about the Nexia Gate. *Questions about your destiny must be directed to an oracle,* she had said. Maybe Selene could explain what the prophecy really meant for him. Because it seemed, especially after dinner the night before, that there was a lot about it that he didn't know.

They returned to the river and boarded the ferry, not needing a coin to depart. Back in the Charion station, they followed another arched passageway, along with a few other vampires. It ended at a wide staircase that spiraled upward out of sight.

They wound up and up, feeling the air slowly warm. Here and there, passageways led off into darkness, and the staircase became narrower. Finally the stairs ended at a wall with a stone door. Oliver pushed it open and they entered a cramped hallway. Flickering candles hung on the walls between hollowed-out niches that held collapsed piles of bones.

"Hey, catacombs," said Dean. "Nice."

There was a pattering of unseen rats' feet, and a smell of old bones and moist earth. Oliver led the way, following the trail of candles through the maze of narrow tunnels. Every now and then, a small set of stairs brought them a few feet closer to the surface. Soon the floor became tiled with flat stones, and the recesses in the walls were replaced by polished marble plaques bearing ancient symbols and names in Latin. Oliver took a final turn, ascended a steep staircase, and reached a tight room with crypts on either side. Pushing through a squealing iron door, the two emerged into the warm summer night.

They stood in an ancient graveyard of mausoleums, tombstones, and shrines. A gentle hill sloped down to a small stone church. Its stained-glass windows flickered with warm light. Beyond that was a little road, bounding through farmland. A town glowed in the distance.

"That's Fortuna," said Oliver. He reached into his pocket and produced the tiny toy television. "All right . . ." He twisted the yellow dial forward four times, then twice back, then said, "Emalie."

The TV didn't change, or emit a light, or anything.

"Did it work?" Dean asked.

Oliver shrugged. "Maybe Emalie's still working the kinks out."

Excuse me?

"Whu?" Oliver looked around wildly.

"What?" asked Dean.

"Did you hear —"

I'm in here. It was Emalie. *Duh, in your head.*

"Oh," Oliver said aloud. "Hi." He turned to Dean and tapped a finger to his temple. "She's in here."

Dean frowned. "How come I can't hear her?" he whined.

Tell him I'm sorry. The charm only works on the one who activates it. It invites me in.

"She says it's 'cause I'm special," said Oliver.

Dean looked shocked. "Did you just make a joke?"

Oliver felt a rush of embarrassment and shook his head dismissively. "All right, now what, Emalie?"

"Hey, Emalie," Dean went on, "if you can hear me, I think your charm messed up Oliver's head. He just tried to be funny."

"Tsss," Oliver hissed.

What's he talking about? Emalie asked.

Um, thought Oliver, desperate to change the subject from Emalie's charm. *Where are you?*

Not far from you. Follow the road toward town.

Oliver and Dean weaved through the graves to the road, then walked toward the distant glow. Behind them, the moon hung low on the horizon, still tinted amber. The road was quiet. Only an occasional tiny car zipped by, its tires slapping on the old cobblestones. They walked on the dirt shoulder, beside an ancient stone wall that was waist high and overgrown with vines and shrubs. Rolling fields stretched away on either side of the road. Here and there in the fields stood solitary ruins: a tower, a lone archway, the crumbling remains of a building, all relics of the Romans. An occasional villa was nestled within a cluster of trees, its windows aglow.

As they walked, Oliver began to notice an odd flickering out of the corner of his eye. At first, he thought he was imagining it, but then he stopped and peered into the tangles of vegetation on the wall and saw tiny flashes of pale light, a green-tinted yellow. Each light would move for a moment, then wink out, appearing a moment later.

"What?" asked Dean.

"Those lights," Oliver whispered. "It seems to be some kind of energy or enchantment —"

"Dude." Dean chuckled. "You're a comedian tonight. Those are just fireflies."

"What are they?"

"Really? You've never seen fireflies before? They're insects that glow. They use the light to attract mates. I guess you don't really see them in Seattle."

"Or underground," added Oliver.

"True."

They continued walking, and Oliver slowly got used to the tiny blinking insect lights. He noticed more of them among the grassy fields and in the shadows of the trees beyond.

The farms began to give way to groups of houses. Ahead, the outskirts of town became visible. There were clusters of buildings with a few lights on, the blue glow and babble of a television from a window here and there, and the murmur and clinking of people eating and drinking outside.

Over here, said Emalie moments later.

A small driveway led away from the road. It was lined with old trees. They followed it to a gate displaying a gold sign that read: *Luogo Storico: Fortuna Antica.* Oliver and Dean vaulted over the gate. They passed a gift shop, closed for the evening, and found themselves on an ancient road of large, uneven cobblestones. On either side were crumbled walls of the ancient Roman ruins of Fortuna. The walls created a checkerboard of square rooms, their floors given over to grass. An occasional marble column reached up toward the original heights of what had once been tall villas, only to end jaggedly, its top long since collapsed.

One structure still stood tall: a wide, curved amphitheater with arches around its perimeter.

"Kind of looks like that Colosseum you see in pictures of Rome," Dean observed.

In here, said Emalie.

Oliver and Dean ducked under an archway. A short tunnel led them out to the floor. A half-moon of stone seats arced around them. They stood in the space that was once a stage.

"Hey, boys." Emalie was sitting halfway up the steps in a T-shirt and jeans. She stood and hopped down, slinging her shoulder bag. "So how's things?"

"All right," Oliver replied, trying to think of something more interesting to say.

"Oliver's family is crraa-zy," Dean reported with a smile. He went on to recap their arrival in Morosia and the awkward dinner.

"Sounds rough." Emalie eyed Oliver with concern.

"Eh." Oliver shrugged. "Whatever. Just the usual, I guess." As he spoke, a firefly floated by his face, distracting him with its blinking.

"Also, Oliver thinks his parents might sacrifice him tomorrow night," Dean added casually.

"What?" Emalie exclaimed.

"Yeah, about that . . ." Oliver recounted the conversation he'd overheard back in his house.

"And then," said Dean, "this girl Lythia told us that tomorrow night is seventh moon. That was the night that Selene got her prophecy. Oh, and Selene is Oliver's oracle."

"Who's Lythia?" Emalie asked immediately.

"She's just some vampire girl," said Oliver.

"Like our age but with a demon, and she won all this money at roulette," Dean continued.

Emalie's brow puckered. "Well, she sounds special. This Lythia didn't happen to tell you where to *find* Selene, did she?"

Oliver shrugged. "No."

"Well, we haven't been able to find out, either," said Emalie. "My aunt and I have researched the town records, asked around, and nobody knows anything about a Selene. We don't even know if she's in town, and we don't know why my mom wanted to see her." Emalie frowned. "It's turning into a dead end. The only thing I found was references to Selene in Greek myths. That was the name of a moon goddess."

"That makes sense with what Désirée said, right?" mused Dean. "The whole *'light that burns cold'* thing?"

"Mmm . . ." Oliver paused, suddenly distracted. He turned and was surprised to see a number of fireflies blinking together around a marble pillar base nearby. The pillar itself had fallen over and lay cracked into segments on the ground. As Oliver watched, more fireflies slowly gravitated toward this tablelike structure. They spiraled above it, forming a lazy tornado of pale light. And many were landing on the surface, crawling over one another in a tight mass. They seemed to be very interested in something lying there. Oliver started walking toward them.

"And what is an oracle, anyway?" Dean was asking. "A vampire, zombie shaman, wraith, or, like, a god or something?"

"I don't think we're looking for a god," Emalie said. "We — Oliver?"

"Check this out." Oliver had reached the pedestal, the many spiraling fireflies casting a greenish glow on his face. His hand flicked out and he caught one, then watched the little pill-shaped creature crawl along his white palm, its light blinking like a distress call. The bug reached the tip of his thumb and flew to rejoin the others.

Oliver reached into the swirl of little creatures and picked up the piece of paper they seemed so interested in. As his fingers touched it, all the fireflies shot into the air and began to scatter.

Emalie and Dean appeared beside him. "What's that?" Emalie asked.

"It looks like a brochure," said Oliver.

"It must have food on it, or something that's attracting the bugs," Emalie mused.

Oliver turned the glossy paper over in his hand. The writing was in Italian, the cover reading: *Museo Storico di Fortuna*. There was nothing special about it.

"That's for the historical museum in town," said Emalie.

"Nothing important, I guess." Oliver handed it to her.

"Did you think it would be?" Dean asked.

"No," said Oliver, except, for some reason, he kind of had. "Sorry." He shook his head. "Okay, so now what —"

"Hold on . . ." said Emalie hoarsely. She was staring intently at the back side of the brochure, her hand starting to shake.

"What?" Dean leaned over to look. "Huh, that's funny. That looks like you."

Oliver saw a picture of a tall statue. It was a woman carved in white stone, dressed in flowing robes and frozen in mid-stride.

"Not me . . ." Emalie whispered. "Th — that's my mom."

CHAPTER 8

The Mystery of Phoebe

Emalie didn't speak until they were almost to the center of Fortuna. As they followed the road through the outskirts of town, passing sleeping villas and apartments, she strode ahead of them, clutching the brochure tightly.

"What do you think that's about," Dean murmured to Oliver, "with the statue?"

"No idea," Oliver replied.

"Do you think it has something to do with Selene?"

Oliver shrugged. It seemed important to find out either way.

As they walked, Oliver thought more about Selene. He knew he wanted to talk to her, but he still wasn't exactly sure what about. He already knew his destiny, and what it involved, so really, what else was there? *There might be details that no one's told you.* What details? He didn't know . . . but then a new thought made its way to the surface of his brain: *Maybe if Selene can tell you more about the prophecy, then you'll really want to fulfill it.*

Yes, with a rush of anxiety, Oliver found himself facing a truth that might have been his biggest problem: Sure, he didn't like learning, as he had last winter, that he was secretly being prepared for a prophecy, or that he was being lied to, but really, what was *wrong* with having been chosen to save the vampires? Was there a vampire kid out there who would *really* be upset to find out that he was going to be a hero?

Well, yes, there was one: Oliver. Because the truth was, he didn't *want* his destiny. And he knew that, despite the lies and the secrets, any normal vampire would have. That made him feel the most ashamed, and the most alone. But he couldn't help it. Being free from Earth meant leaving behind Emalie and Dean . . . *and my human parents, if they really are alive.* . . . He didn't want that. And he didn't want the pressure, or the responsibility, or any of it. So maybe talking to Selene could help somehow.

"Here we are," said Emalie. They had reached a crowded piazza. Oliver looked up to see the marble front of the historical museum. Two staircases climbed at angles toward the front door. In the triangle of space between them was a fountain of white stone. Streams of clear water, illuminated with yellow lights, cascaded down a series of ledges to a blue pool. At the top of the fountain was a statue of Neptune, wrapped in robes and pointing his trident outward. The windows of the museum were dark.

Oliver saw many couples around the fountain, holding hands or sitting on its edges. Boys darted from one to the next, trying to sell roses. There were gaggles of tourists, some throwing coins in the fountain, some doing strange human things like videotaping the running water or taking pictures of themselves in front of it. He noticed a solitary vampire off to the side, standing before a beat-up easel, painting the scene, which seemed like a much more meaningful way to experience it.

Cafés lined the sides of the piazza, their tables packed with human diners sitting beneath umbrellas. The leaning buildings above them had their shutters thrown open to the hot night, with curtains billowing out around fans on porches. There was a din of conversation and clinking cutlery, along with the strong scent of wine and food, which helped to temper the less pleasant smell of sweaty humans.

"So, in?" said Dean, starting toward the staircase beside the fountain. He stopped when neither Emalie nor Oliver moved. "What's up?"

"Just . . . a little freaked out," said Emalie. "What's with you, Oliver?"

Oliver motioned to the fountain. "Just a sec . . . nine hundred seventy-three — four — five — six . . . have to count the coins . . ."

Dean rolled his eyes at Emalie. "Right. Oliver's got this going on, too. I love how vampires think humans and zombies are the ones with the issues."

Oliver's shoulders heaved. "Okay. Four thousand three hundred and twelve," he announced.

They started around the fountain beside the café tables. Suddenly a hand reached out and grabbed Oliver's shirt. "Well, if it isn't little cousin Oliver!" Oliver turned to find Misère and Gustav sitting at a café table, a wineglass in front of each and a carafe of blood between them. A quick glance around told Oliver that this was one of the cafés that had a vampire menu, if you knew which waiter to ask.

Misère's long hair was pushed all across to one side of her face, falling down over a white silk dress. Her face was pristinely powdered, her eyes ringed in black eyeliner, her lips painted purple. Gustav was huddled in an olive-green military jacket and a black beret that he'd reportedly gotten during a civil war in Chad.

Misère looked over at Emalie and Dean and smiled. "Bane told us you were disturbed," she said, turning to

Gustav. "What should we make of this, Gus? It's so repulsive I almost find it interesting."

Gustav shrugged. "Fascinating," he said, smiling at Emalie. "Dinner on one side, servant on the other. So efficient."

"These are my cousins," Oliver muttered to Emalie.

"He's no more peculiar than his brother," Misère noted, scowling.

Oliver looked around. "Where is Bane?"

Gustav nodded his chin toward the museum. "He's still in there. Who knows what's keeping him? We've been sitting out here waiting to cause some mayhem for half an hour now."

"Why even go in there in the first place?" Misère pouted. "To feed on the one security guard? We took care of him in moments, but then your brother goes and takes off after some curator lady. You Nocturnes are unhinged, and not in the pleasing way."

"It almost makes me want to say that Dad is right about these New World headcases," added Gustav. "So, Oliver, where are you and your *things* off to?"

"Into the museum," Oliver replied flatly.

"Ha! That's hilarious!" Gustav chuckled.

"Yeah," said Oliver, "hilarious."

"Well, if you see your brother in there," said Misère, "tell him your cousins are about to leave, as they are bored beyond belief." She took a sip of her blood, slouched back in her chair, and cast a disinterested stare across the piazza.

The three moved on, climbing the steps. Oliver glanced back at the fountain with every sound of a splashing coin, getting an updated count. Ahead, one of the tall metal doors stood slightly ajar. Oliver sniffed the air and caught a pungent odor. "Careful," he whispered, then pushed open the door.

The entry hall was dark. Ahead, a body was sprawled across the marble floor. "He's dead," Oliver reported immediately. As they neared, they could see the uniform of the security guard and the bloodstained collar. Oliver could tell by the scent that Misère had done the killing. He and Dean continued for a moment before realizing that Emalie wasn't with them. They turned back to see her standing over the man, looking down, hands shoved in her jeans pockets.

"He had four kids," she said quietly, eyes closed. "He — he was saving money. Hoping to take them to the beach later this summer." Emalie's voice cracked. "Hoping to get along with them better . . ." She sniffled. "It's too soon . . . so much he still wants to say . . ." Emalie grabbed her ears. "He's shouting for them . . . so loudly . . . but they won't hear him. . . ."

"Come on, Emalie," Dean called. "Nothing we can do." He leaned into Oliver's ear. "Actually, I'm starving," he confided. Oliver guessed that Dean was imagining having a spare moment to procure a true zombie dinner, since the security guard wouldn't mind at this point.

Emalie shivered, then stepped around the body and caught up with them.

"How do you know those things about him?" asked Oliver.

"I . . . it's hard to describe. I could just feel it around him."

"But he's dead," said Dean.

"I know," said Emalie. "That's new. With living people, I can read their energy like that — you know, their hopes and fears."

"And tell the future from it," added Oliver, leading them up a flight of stairs to another hall. He had picked up Bane's scent ahead. "That's an Orani's most valuable skill."

"I can't really do that yet." Emalie frowned. "And it doesn't feel valuable. More like sad."

"But so what about just now?" asked Dean. "A dead guy doesn't have a future."

"No, but he did until a few minutes ago. It's like the essence of his living self is still around him. I think it takes some time to leave. With a living person, I have to use a charm to get in their heads, and it's like I'm looking out their eyes . . . but this time it happened outside his body. I could hear him, in agony . . . and there was something . . . white."

"White?" asked Dean.

"Yeah. Not sure what I mean by that, maybe it was his spirit, or —"

"*Shh.*" Oliver had been listening intently to the conversation — these abilities that Emalie had were much bigger than she knew, bigger even than Oliver totally understood — but now he heard voices.

The hallway they were following had opened on one side. Archways overlooked a long room, three stories tall. Oliver, Emalie, and Dean were on the middle floor. Paintings covered the walls in a patchwork display, and white statues stood on the marble floor below. High above was an arched glass ceiling. The moon hung in the center of one of the large panes.

A voice hissed from below: "Let me make this a little more clear . . ." It was Bane. There was a sickly sound of cracking bone and a shrill, wincing cry.

Peering into the dark, Oliver spied Bane down on the floor, holding a middle-aged woman up in the air by the throat. His other hand had just elicited that crack of bone from one of her fingers. The woman was gasping for breath, oval glasses askew in front of wide, terrified eyes.

"You're going to tell me where she is," Bane went on, "or we're going to follow this little address on your business card home, and me and my cousins —

who are very, very hungry — are going to find out if you have any lovely *bambini* sleeping peacefully in their beds. . . ."

"*No, prego, no!*" the woman cried.

"Where is *Selene*?" Bane hissed.

"Dude," Dean whispered, "your brother is looking for Selene, too?"

Oliver was stunned, or was he? There had been that time in the library, back in February, when Oliver had caught Bane talking to the Codex that knew about the Nexia Gate. . . . Later in the spring, Oliver had gone back to that same Codex to ask his own questions about the Nexia Gate, only to find that the Codex had been *removed* for maintenance. It had not returned as of June. *Why would Bane want to find the oracle who told my prophecy? And what did he find out that day?*

But Oliver wondered now if maybe there was actually an easy explanation for what Bane was up to. Maybe he was jealous. It made sense, didn't it? Maybe Bane had been learning about Oliver's prophecy because *he* wished that he was the chosen vampire. That would explain why he was always so mean to Oliver. Maybe he made fun of Oliver being different because he wished he was. Maybe it made him crazy that their parents had chosen Oliver, the weak one, instead of Bane, the stronger, more dangerous one. . . .

And so maybe Bane had been a step ahead of Oliver all along. Maybe he'd found out about Selene from the Codex in the library and knew that she was near Morosia. Maybe he'd been using his time out with the cousins to track her down, and that had led him to the curator.

"Tell me!" Bane shouted.

"Oliver," Emalie whispered. "We have to stop him."

Dean grabbed the edge of the railing. "Let's get down there."

Oliver threw an arm in front of him. "Hold on." His first instinct was just like Dean's: to leap off this balcony and tackle Bane, then maybe grab a nearby statue and hit him with it. . . . The problem was, after the moment of surprise, Oliver and Dean would be no match for Bane. And as soon as Bane saw them, he might assume they were looking for Selene, too. Knowing Bane, he would do something like kill the curator just to keep them from getting any information. If only there was a way to find out what they needed to know without Bane even realizing . . .

Oliver turned to Emalie. "Can you get into her head and find out what she knows?"

Emalie nodded. "Pretty sure." She reached to her neck and pulled a silver chain from her shirt. At the end was a ruby-colored oval, round on one side and carved like a beetle on the other.

Oliver recognized it immediately. "Cool, a scarab. What dynasty?" he asked, referring to its Egyptian origin.

"Old Kingdom," said Emalie. "This one's got a conduit charm in it. It can link me to her."

There was another hideous cracking sound from below and a fresh scream from the curator.

Emalie placed the conduit between her palms, then pressed them together in front of her face. She closed her eyes and blew between her hands. There was the faintest glow of red, and Emalie seemed to slump.

Dean snapped in front of her face. Emalie didn't respond at all. "Where is she?"

Oliver turned back to the railing. "Down there." They watched as Bane shook the curator. "In her head."

"Last chance, *signora bella* . . ." Bane pulled the curator close. "*Dicami dove trovare Selene.*"

"Kinda surprised he knows Italian," murmured Dean.

"Probably got it from his demon," Oliver explained. "They usually bring along a handful of languages, since they've been around for so long." Oliver gripped the railing, watching. If Emalie was successful, Bane would never know she was in there —

Suddenly the woman's eyes hardened. Her free hand shot to Bane's neck. Her mouth opened and the voice that came out sounded as if it had been piped through an enormous, echoing hallway.

"*Siete il guasto allineare!*" the curator screamed.

Bane recoiled. He tossed the curator away. She sprawled across the floor, hit her head against the base of the wall, and slumped over, unconscious.

"What just happened?" asked Dean.

"Guh!" Emalie returned, her shoulders thrusting with a huge intake of breath.

Oliver watched as Bane warily approached the curator. He looked shaken. When he found her out cold, he turned and started to leave — yet stopped, sniffing the air. Oliver ducked back, pressing Dean and Emalie into the shadows . . . but Bane continued out. Oliver kept still until his scent faded. He turned to Emalie.

She was still catching her breath, but had an excited smile. "Wow," she said. "Okay, the statue is that way." She pointed down the hall.

"What about Selene?" Dean asked.

"I'm not sure, but Francesca — that's the curator — was thinking about the statue when Bane asked her about Selene. Let's go —"

"Emalie," Oliver interrupted. "What did you say to Bane?"

"Oh, that . . ." Emalie looked away and shrugged. "I'm not really sure. . . . Okay, so I got into Francesca's head and it was really tight in there, 'cause she was so scared. . . . I was seeing out her eyes, into Bane's — that was freaky — and something, I don't know, clicked."

"What do you mean, clicked?" asked Oliver.

"Like, for a second, I could sort of see into your brother's head, too. I felt this big, well, I guess it was fear inside him, and it was like suddenly I connected their minds together. This big fear in Bane's head came flashing across into the curator's head, and so it flooded over me. It felt really freaky, so I pushed it back out, and then Francesca just yelled it: *You are the true failure.*"

"What's that mean?" wondered Dean.

Emalie shrugged. "You'd have to ask Bane. It was his fear. Anyway, he freaked, and I got thrown out of Francesca's head when she was knocked out."

Oliver wondered what this all meant. Why would Bane feel like he was a failure? Maybe it had to do with his jealousy, as Oliver suspected: He felt like a failure for not being the chosen vampire.

Emalie was starting down the hall. "Come on," she said brightly. Oliver couldn't help noticing how excited she seemed after her harrowing trip into the curator's mind. It reminded him of how vampires could get a blood high: like a sugar rush in a human.

They hurried back down to the first floor and entered a smaller exhibit room. The room was lined with a series of heads sculpted from black metal. These were the busts of Roman emperors. A few had white eyes made of marble, but in most the eyes were missing, leaving hollow spaces. There was a single large painting on each wall, and in the center of the room was the statue.

The woman stood in stride, wearing flowing robes, her long hair waving over her shoulders. One arm was bent in front of her, holding up a flat object. It had a short handle and a diamond-shaped top. It looked like a hand mirror.

Emalie halted directly in front of the statue. She gazed up at the face, her lip quivering.

Oliver and Dean walked around to the side of the pedestal, where a plaque explained the statue in English and Italian.

"This is Phoebe," Oliver said, scanning the plaque. "The artist is unknown, but it was found in Tempiale di Necromancy, which is somewhere nearby." Oliver read on. "Phoebe was a moon goddess, often associated with . . ."

"Selene," Dean finished. He looked over at Emalie. "Does she look like —"

"So much," Emalie whispered, as if she feared awakening the statue. Her gaze remained locked on its face.

Oliver stepped back, taking in the tall marble form, smooth stone face, and blank eyes. . . . He felt a presence rush through him. They were close to something here, but what?

Dean was trying to piece it together. "So, there's a statue that looks like your mom," he said quietly from beside Emalie, "and the statue's named Phoebe, which is a name for the moon goddess. And the moon goddess can also be named Selene. Does this mean that your mom *is* Selene?"

Emalie glanced at him uncertainly, biting her lip in thought.

"And how could a statue from, like, thousands of years ago look like your mom?"

"I don't know," Emalie whispered.

Oliver kept staring at the statue, moving behind it to get a better look at that diamond-shaped object she was holding. It did look like it was supposed to be a mirror —

Oliver spied something else in that hand. Something stuffed in a small space between the grasping fingers and the handle . . . something that wasn't part of the sculpture.

Without really thinking about it, he leaped up onto the rectangular pedestal and grabbed Phoebe's waist for support —

A high-pitched electronic whine flooded the room.

"Dude, what are you doing?" Oliver barely heard Dean shout from below. To his sensitive ears, the museum's alarm was practically deafening.

Wincing, Oliver reached forward and plucked the tiny object from the cool, smooth statue hand. He jumped to the floor, landing behind the statue and shoving the object in his pocket.

"We should probably be leaving!" Dean shouted, starting out of the room. Emalie began backing out after him, her eyes still fixated on the statue's face.

Oliver was about to follow them, but now something else about the statue caught his eye. On the back of its rectangular base, in the shadow beneath the raised heel of the left foot, there was a tiny scratch mark that most any human would've assumed was the hasty graffiti of some long-ago vandal. To Oliver, it was something much more informative:

Oliver gazed at it for a long moment to be sure of what he was seeing, then raced around to Emalie and Dean. "Let's get to the roof!"

They sprinted back through the hall, yet as they neared the staircase, they heard the pounding of footsteps and shouting voices.

"This way!" Oliver called. They sprinted down another hall and found themselves back in the long, high gallery where the curator still lay unconscious. Oliver looked up, eyeing the railing they'd stood at moments before. There was a railing for a third floor above that. He glanced at Dean and they shared a nod.

They flanked Emalie on either side, grabbed her by the shoulders —

"Hey!"

They leaped upward, shooting to the third-floor balcony, where they landed in a stumbling mass of legs and arms. Straightening themselves out, they continued down a short, low-ceilinged hall with offices on either side. Oliver ran ahead to a stairwell door and found a narrow flight of stairs, which led up to a locked door. He easily slapped it open, and they emerged on the roof, finally free of the high-pitched alarm din.

"Geez," Emalie complained, rubbing her neck. "Can you guys let me know next time you're going to go all superhero, so I can at least brace myself?"

"Sorry," Dean offered. They headed to the back of the building. "Brace yourself," he said, and he and Oliver grabbed Emalie by the shoulders again, this time leaping from the museum to the next roof over. They bounded over three streets before stopping.

"Hang on to me," Oliver instructed. As Emalie did so, Oliver dangled over the side of the building, concentrated on the forces, and scaled down it feetfirst.

"You guys have it rough," said Dean with a smile as he leaped down from one balcony to the next. He landed on the railing of one that had golden light spilling out, and when he glanced inside, his eyes went wide with interest. "Whoa —" He proceeded to lose his concentration and drop like a rock the rest of the way to the quiet, twisting street below. Oliver and Emalie found him sprawled among a pile of trash cans.

"Nice," Oliver joked.

Dean got up, rubbing his head. "It was worth it. There was this lady —"

"I don't want to know," Emalie interrupted, "do I?"

Dean smiled. "Probably not."

Emalie turned seriously to Oliver. "What were you thinking in there, leaping on that statue?"

Oliver reached into his pocket and produced the tiny object. "This was in her hand." In his palm was a small leather strap with a buckle. A single gold bell dangled from it.

"It looks like a pet collar," Emalie mused.

Oliver shrugged. "There was something else: I saw a Skrit symbol on the back of the statue. Any vampire would know it. It's for the Asylum Colony."

"What's that?" Emalie asked.

"Well, it is what it sounds like: an asylum. For the insane, or the dangerous. Morosia's Asylum Colony is, like, the vampire world's most famous one. I think maybe Selene is there." It made sense to Oliver as he thought about it. He didn't know much about the Asylum — nobody in the New World did — but it was likely a safe place to keep an important oracle.

"Can we go there now?" Emalie asked.

"No," Oliver replied. "I don't know where it is. But I can find out easily enough from my family." Oliver knew just the person to ask. But he had a worried thought. "It's a dangerous place. At least, that's what I've heard."

"What else is new?" Emalie retorted. "So, tomorrow night, then?" she asked eagerly.

"Well, yeah," Oliver agreed, knowing there was no use in arguing against her coming. "Can you meet us at those catacombs?"

"Gotcha." Emalie nodded.

Oliver turned to Dean. "Okay. We should get back."

The three parted ways, Oliver and Dean heading out of town toward the cemetery and the catacombs. Oliver felt a steady buzz in his gut. He didn't know what to make of Bane, but he knew where to find Selene, and there was a chance they could get to her before the sacrifice. The sacrifice . . . Maybe Bane knew about that, too, and wanted to take Oliver's place as the chosen child once Oliver was out of the way. . . . It was too much to figure out right now.

All the way back to Morosia, his thoughts continued to swirl, flashing bright and random, like the fireflies in the bushes along the roadside.

CHAPTER 9

Hades' Well

"I was wondering about the Asylum Colony," said Oliver.

Phlox heard him first. She looked up from her espresso slowly, as if every little thing at this point in the visit was more than she could bear. "Why would you wonder about —"

"Yes, yes!" Oliver's words had reached Myrandah, who was pushing a poker into the curved opening of the brick oven. She spun around and waddled across the kitchen, brandishing the red-hot glowing poker in front of her. "Listen to the little darling," she snarled approvingly. "He takes an interest in the proud history despite his upbringing."

Phlox's head dropped back to her espresso. Sebastian had left earlier for some other bit of business. Bane was still asleep. Dominus was out on a walk.

Myrandah dropped the poker in a bucket of water with a hiss. "Come along, Phloxiana," she barked, guiding Oliver across the room. "Does he know of his great-uncle Renfeld, a pioneer of the work at the Colony?"

"No, I don't," Oliver replied, trying to sound as interested as possible. "What did he do there?"

"Why, he studied beneath the great Irving Emerick, though maybe you don't even know of him."

"I do, actually," Oliver replied. He'd heard of Dr. Emerick when learning about the Orani. "He was a doctor of demon bloodlines, wasn't he?"

"Yes." Myrandah opened a door and Oliver and Phlox followed her into a dark room. There was a spark of fire, and Myrandah appeared in the glow of a match. She lit a candelabra on the wall. "The demosapien lines were his specialty. And Renfeld carried out his experiments at the Asylum Colony."

Mounted on the wall in front of them was a tall metal rack that held oil paintings, one beside another, like pages of a book. Myrandah started flipping through the large canvases. Each painting was a portrait of one of Oliver's relatives throughout the ages. She stopped at a dour old man with very little hair and even less skin. He was depicted in a tweed suit. This was the same painting of Great-Uncle Renfeld that Phlox had hung in the abandoned upstairs of Oliver's house, except that in this one, his face looked different. Actually, it looked the same at first, but then as Oliver gazed, the face changed.

The human face was replaced by a green-skinned, glow-ing-eyed demon with razor teeth. This was a representation of the demon within the vampire. These demon-revealing paintings could only be made in the Underworld.

"Ahh," Myrandah said, gazing at the painting. "He was such a careful student. Working night and day."

"You must have been proud of him," said Oliver, try-ing to be polite. He couldn't break his gaze from the demon face.

"We felt pride," Myrandah began, but then her tone soured. "But how the New World scientists distorted his work."

"Here we go," Phlox sighed.

"His studies twisted and corrupted!"

Oliver worried that his chance to learn about the Asylum Colony was slipping away. "I — I thought the Asylum Colony was a prestigious place."

"Oh, naturally it is. Their research has always been pure, but see how the likes of the Half-Light Consortium have misused it. . . ."

"Okay, Mother," grumbled Phlox.

"I'd still like to see the Colony," said Oliver.

"Bah." Myrandah waved her hand dismissively. "It's too far a walk for these old legs."

"And too far for you to go," said Phlox. "We need you around tonight, Oliver."

"Um, okay," Oliver replied with fresh worry. Did they want him around in time for the seventh moon sacrifice? "I was just going to go upstairs to hang out with Dean for a little while."

"Just make sure you're back for dinner," said Phlox tersely. She left the room.

Oliver heard Myrandah sigh. He turned to see that she had flipped along in the paintings, and was now looking at a younger woman, in her late teens, standing regally in a white satin dress, her platinum hair falling in splendid curls down her shoulders. Oliver realized that it was Phlox, as a newly sired vampire. She looked about Misère's age. The image was shocking. He'd never imagined his mother so young, her face so lineless, her eyes so big . . .

Yet as he watched, Phlox's eyes turned into gleaming turquoise slits, more reptilian than human. Her pale face transformed into deep, leathery yellow skin with tiny purple spikes lining her forehead and chin. Her delicate lips dissolved into a mouth of glistening black-glass teeth. This was the demon, the true *vampyr,* inside Oliver's mother.

"Such a lovely girl," Myrandah said softly.

Oliver just stared. There was nothing like that inside him yet. But someday there would be. Would he change, as Bane had? Become a different person? He wondered if he wanted that, and wasn't sure. And then he wondered: When he opened the Gate, this *vampyr* inside him would be free again, but would that be *Oliver* anymore? Would he still be himself, free in another dimension, or only partly Oliver, or not Oliver at all? Vampires like Phlox weren't bothered by this idea, were they? Probably not. It wasn't like a vampire to think about consequences — to think about *what if*, but Oliver always did. It was almost like everything he thought was different than what the rest of his world was thinking . . .

"Dear boy . . ." Oliver was startled by Myrandah's voice. His gaze broke from Phlox's image, and he found his stooped grandmother standing quite close to him, peering into his face, her eyes glowing, not with anger, but with emotion. "So much that young Oliver never asked for . . ."

"Huh?" Oliver asked, but he'd heard her, and he agreed.

"See him wonder about his purpose. Purpose he never chose . . ." Oliver felt relief at hearing this, though he tried not to show it. "He craves only a normal vampire's existence . . ."

Oliver shrugged. He wasn't sure if that was really true, but he tried not to show that, either. He had very little clue at the moment what to show, or not show, or even to think.

Now Myrandah's wiry hand touched his. Oliver felt something soft between her talon-like fingernails. He looked down to see her pressing a small scrap of parchment into his hand. Oliver held it up and saw that it was a hand-drawn map . . . to the Asylum Colony.

"This may be of use," Myrandah finished, then turned back to the painting. "Go," she said over her shoulder. Oliver took a last glance at Phlox's *vampyr* face, and hurried out.

Reaching the roof, he found a pack of zombies chasing after an old leather soccer ball, tackling one another violently in pursuit. At each end, instead of goals, there seemed to be other zombies tied to tall posts.

"Hey, Oliver!" In fact, Dean was currently playing the position of being tied to a post. Now a male player broke free from the pack, dribbling the ball toward Dean. Howling zombies closed in behind him.

"Shoot!" a woman screamed. The zombie man scooped the ball up in his hand, planted his feet, and hurled it with incredible force right at Dean. Dean winced and the soccer ball slammed him in the shoulder.

"Shoulder only!" a referee shouted. "Three points!"

There were howls of disappointment and joy from the players. Dean seemed relieved.

Oliver sat on the edge of the roof until the game ended. He looked out over the smoking warmth of Morosia. With the torchlight throughout the city and the large cauldron fire atop Tartarus, the city always looked as if it had just been sacked and left ablaze. There was something soothing about that. Oliver could see the smoke and heat gathering near the roof of the enormous cavern and slipping up a giant hole in the ceiling — a lava tube that vented on the side of the volcano, Mt. Morta, high above.

"Phew. Rough game." Dean dropped down beside him, rubbing his shoulder. With a crack, he pushed the dislocated arm bone back into its socket. "Being goalie is tough, but we won!" he said brightly. "It's funny 'cause goalie is what I played in human soccer, and I was terrible. It's kinda nice to be good at something."

"How are you *good* at being tied to a pole?" Oliver asked.

"Well, I didn't get hit in the head," Dean explained. "A head shot is worth ten points. Some say it's all luck, but it also takes the right amount of shifting, you know, ever so slightly this way and that, and psyching out your opponent with your eyes." Dean made an odd, concentrating face. "Anyway . . . did you get the goods?"

"Yeah." Oliver held out the map. "Ready to go?"

"Ooh, yeah, just a sec." Dean headed over to the fire pits, grabbed a sheep-sized leg bone, and rejoined Oliver. "Let's do it."

They followed the same path as the day before, leaving Morosia, Dean slowly grinding down the bone on the way. As they started up the spiral staircase to the surface, Oliver got out the television charm. He had barely finished twisting it when Emalie spoke in his head:

Hey, Oliver.

Hey, where are you?

"Right here, actually." Oliver and Dean looked up to find Emalie coming down the steps. "I got an early start and figured you'd want to meet down here." She was wearing her black sweater and hat, two braids falling from it.

Oliver looked at her strangely. "Did anyone see you?" Instinctively, he looked around for Jenette's black shadow.

"Trust me," said Emalie, blowing up at her forehead as if there was hair in her eyes, even though there wasn't, "I didn't call Jenette. Whenever I passed vampires on the stairs, I just concentrated on not being noticed."

"That worked?" Oliver asked.

"Pretty well, actually." Emalie sounded proud of herself.

"Well, cool . . ." Oliver remembered the straw charm that Emalie thought had been protecting her in the Yomi, when really it had been Jenette. Now she didn't need anyone's help? Here was another sign that Emalie's powers were growing.

They proceeded a few revolutions up the stairs, then turned down a narrow hall that twisted through a rock fissure, its uneven walls bowing in and out. There was no ceiling above, only darkness. They reached a staircase that descended, still in the narrow fissure. Every now and then they had to duck beneath outcroppings of rock. The stairs became damp, and Oliver heard a gentle rushing sound like water.

The stairs ended on a ledge along the edge of the black river Acheron. Oliver looked downstream to the right, and in the distance saw the bobbing light of the ferry.

"What is it?" Emalie asked quietly, leaning toward the water.

"Energy . . . forces running between worlds," said Oliver.

"Weird, huh?" said Dean.

Oliver consulted the map, then led the way following the ledge upstream, the strange whispering gurgle of the river keeping them oddly silent. Torches dotted the wall, casting no reflection on the water. A thin wire fence stretched along the river's edge, between iron posts. Oliver found, because of the strange lack of light on the river, he needed to hold the wire for balance.

Soon they reached a wall. A staircase led up into another fissure. Beside them, the river emerged from a curved tunnel. At the top of the stairs, they followed another narrow passageway, reached its end in moments, and found themselves at a more substantial stone railing.

"Whoa," breathed Emalie, looking up.

They were on a ring-shaped stone platform, along the wall of a cylindrical chasm that climbed into darkness both above and below. Oliver had never been here before, but he'd heard about it. The whisper of the river echoed, unseen, from below.

The trio looked up, down, to either side, avoiding looking straight ahead until finally there was nowhere else to gaze. Pale white light shimmered faintly on their faces.

"So . . ." Dean said, his attempt at sounding casual betrayed by the shaking of his voice.

"This is what the Underground back in Seattle is made to look like," Oliver explained. "They built a chasm, and then put in a waterfall to represent this. . . ." He nodded toward what was in front of them. "They call it Hades' Well."

"What *are* they?" Emalie asked quietly.

"They're spirits," Oliver replied, "of the dead."

Before them, a silent flow of pale, greenish light dropped down the chasm. Within the iridescent current were impressions of faces, stretched like ghosts. The glow reminded Oliver of firefly light.

Dean reached curiously across the railing, but the moment his outstretched fingers touched the falling light, there was a dazzling shock of electrified energy. "Ow!" He pulled his hand back, wincing. "What's with that?"

Oliver shook his head. "You can't touch them." As a zombie, Dean couldn't feel, as Oliver could, the overwhelming sense that you wouldn't *want* to touch them. "They're dead. They're not part of this world anymore."

"Shouldn't I be confused by that?" asked Dean, flexing his hand. "I mean, *we're* dead, right?"

Oliver nodded. It was something a vampire just knew, but how to explain it. . . . "It's the difference between the *un*dead, like us, and the truly dead. We're still connected to this world. These people are fully dead, and so their spirits are free to leave."

"Where are they going?" Emalie asked, her eyes wide, reflecting the green.

"Out into the larger universe," Oliver mused. "They'll go wherever they're drawn . . . like maybe to another world, or back into this world as part of a new life." Oliver watched the pale forms passing by. Their blank faces might have looked sad to a human, but to him, they looked at peace. He was surprised to find that he felt a bit of envy. And he remembered that this feeling of envy was the entire reason for his destiny. "This is the freedom that Half-Light is after," he said, putting the thoughts together. "They want me to open the Gate so that we can be free to leave these bodies behind and travel into the larger universe. Kind of like this, only as demons we could choose where we go."

"Sounds kind of scary," Dean commented, still rubbing his hand.

"Don't you ever wonder what it would be like?" Oliver asked quietly.

"What, being all the way dead? Probably less skin mold," Dean mused.

"Seriously," said Oliver quietly. "You know, to be at peace and free."

Emalie turned to him. "That's weird that you would describe it like that."

"What do you mean?"

"Well, that's what humans are always trying to get, you know? I mean, they're not trying to be dead, but they're always trying to achieve peace and freedom. They never do, though."

"They do when they die," Oliver mused.

Emalie shook her head. "But we don't know that for sure."

"Come on, Oliver," added Dean, "you don't really want to be *dead* dead, do you?"

Oliver thought about it. "I guess not. I feel like I want *something* different, though."

"But vampires have all the freedom in the world," Dean continued. "You practically live forever — you've got no conscience — you can do whatever. You don't even have a master."

Oliver almost laughed. "Don't I? My whole life is being controlled by people and things I don't even understand. Destiny sucks."

"I wouldn't mind having a destiny."

Oliver turned to Dean and almost smiled. "I'd trade you."

Emalie gasped. They turned to find her staring into the flow of spirits, her eyes wide.

"What?" Oliver asked.

"It's him. . . ." she whispered. "The security guard."

Oliver peered into the blur of faces and caught a glimpse of his wide, bearded face, painted in white and green. The blood was gone from his neck.

"Quiet now," said Emalie absently. "His spirit was so loud last night in the museum, so upset . . . but now the sound is gone. I don't know whether that's sad or happy."

Oliver shrugged. "For who?"

"For him, for his kids, his wife . . ."

As Oliver watched the still face slide by, he became aware of yet another sound, this one a smooth humming.

They looked up to find a light high on the wall, lowering toward them. In moments, an oval-shaped glass elevator came into view, sliding along a seam in the rock, its curved glass distorting the reflections of the spirits.

The humming slowed and the elevator reached the ledge where Oliver, Emalie, and Dean stood. Oliver turned to Emalie, only to find that she'd disappeared.

I'm right here. Oliver felt a nudge on his other shoulder. He turned and saw Emalie in the corner of his eye, but then when he looked directly beside him, she wasn't there.

I was going to ask you to do that thing where you're not noticed, Oliver thought to her.

It's pretty good, right? she thought back.

"Stop doing that!" groaned Dean.

Oliver turned to find Dean looking right at where Emalie supposedly was. "You can see her?"

"Yup." Dean waved at her. "Yet another advantage of being a lowly zombie."

"All right." Oliver led the way to the elevator. "That's the way to the Asylum." Its doors were quietly rolling open. A group of vampires emerged, all adults dressed in antique suits, the men with bow ties, the women in skirt-jacket combinations like Oliver vaguely remembered folks wearing when he was very young. An elevator operator in a gray uniform remained behind, sitting on a stool, his hand on the wheel that opened the doors.

"I thought the Colony was in *lower* Morosia?" Dean asked.

"Yeah," Oliver replied. "In the Old World, the surface world is considered 'lower' than the Underworld. Like less powerful, less important."

They were just about to start into the elevator when Oliver felt another tap on his shoulder. *What now?* he thought, turning.

"Hello, Oliver." Sebastian stood beside him.

"D-Dad," Oliver stammered, stunned. *Hide!* he thought frantically to Emalie.

Don't worry, I am.

"H-hey, Mr. Nocturne," Dean offered nervously.

Sebastian glanced at Dean before continuing. "What brings you two out this way?"

"Oh, um." Oliver's thoughts raced. "Gram told us about the Well, so we were just checking it out."

"How fortunate," said Sebastian mildly. "I was looking for you. Come along."

"Oh, but Dean and I were going to —"

Sebastian put his arm across Oliver's shoulders and led him into the elevator. They turned and Dean started to enter —

"Sorry, Dean . . ." Sebastian reached out and firmly pushed Dean away.

"Hey, what —"

Sebastian's tone remained calm. "Oliver and I have some business to attend to," he said, and turned to the operator. "Top level, please." The operator spun his metal wheel, and the doors slid closed.

"He'll find his way home," said Sebastian. He reached into his pocket for a tip for the operator, and as he did, Oliver saw a flash of leather within his long black coat, like the handle of a Stiletto. . . .

The elevator began to rise. Oliver watched helplessly as Dean's face slipped out of sight.

Chapter 10

The Confrontation

Neither Nocturne spoke. Oliver glanced up to see Sebastian staring out the window, the light of the Well making a watery pattern of green on his inscrutable face. Looking down, Oliver saw Dean growing smaller and smaller.

The elevator continued its smooth ascent.

"Where are we going?" Oliver asked nervously, staring straight ahead into the blur of spirit faces.

"The same place you were already headed," Sebastian replied.

"To the Asylum Colony?" Oliver figured it was a waste of time to try lying about that.

Sebastian nodded.

"Why?" Oliver asked.

Sebastian took a moment. "Something needs to be done."

The elevator hummed.

< 150 >

Is this it? Oliver thought horribly. *Is this where I'm turned to dust?* It was seventh moon, after all. He wanted to run, jump, anything: but of course, there was nowhere to go. So instead, he stood there, panicking. He felt like he had his back against a giant, heavy door. He was holding it shut, and from behind it he could hear the babble of many anxious voices — all his worries and fears, too many to count. He just wanted to let them out, to start shouting at his dad, but instead he was just ignoring them all. It was the only way. Except that it was all he could do to keep the door closed. He felt like it might slam him forward. . . .

Try this one first.

It was Emalie. *Are you in here?* Oliver asked, resisting the urge to glance around the elevator.

No, I'm still with Dean, but . . .

Oliver got it. *You're in my head.*

Kinda.

Oliver felt a flush. *I thought you said you needed an invitation?* How often was she able to get inside his head?

Well . . . just listen, Oliver: I can feel your fears. . . . Let me help you. Just start with this one —

What's the use?

Trust me.

Okay. He let the door in his mind slip open a crack and felt a single smooth thought slither out like a tendril of smoke. He could hear the other questions clamoring for his attention, but it was almost like Emalie was acting as a gate and holding them back for him.

"Dad," Oliver began, "where have you been these last couple days?"

"I've been doing work for Half-Light," Sebastian replied, not helping at all.

Now what? Oliver wondered.

Now this one . . . Emalie let another question slip out.

"Does your work have to do with seventh moon?"

"In a sense," said Sebastian.

Oliver looked back out of the elevator. Above, he was just beginning to see a shimmering, waving light at the top of the spirit waterfall.

C'mon, urged Emalie.

What else am I going to say? Oliver thought defeatedly. *He's not going to answer, anyway.*

The elevator slid to a stop. The doors opened, and Oliver and Sebastian stepped out onto another ringed stone platform. Above them, almost within reach, the cascade of spirits seemed to be pouring from a liquid barrier that hung down from a wide hole in the rock ceiling. The barrier was bowed downward like a drop of water about to fall free.

"What is that?" Oliver asked.

"It's the bottom of Lake Naenia, in the crater of Mount Morta. It's a spirit gateway out of the world." Sebastian turned away from the Well. "This way." He started down the single rock passageway. "These tunnels are all old lava tubes," he said as Oliver caught up.

"Huh," said Oliver.

You're stalling . . . Emalie urged.

I am not.

So, what, Emalie sounded annoyed, *you're just going to do the silent brooding thing until you end up turned to dust? Try this.* . . .

Oliver felt the next thought that Emalie suggested slip through. *THAT question? Are you crazy?*

It's what I would do.

Oliver thought about that. Yes, Emalie would. She would ask the biggest question she could think of. Oliver always spent all his energy trying to avoid a big ugly question. He'd rather ask a hundred small ones. Trying it her way sounded horrifying, but maybe at this point it was the only way. . . .

"So," Oliver began as they walked down the tunnel, "you're going to slay me?"

Sebastian stopped in his tracks. He turned to Oliver. "What?"

Oliver couldn't believe he'd said it. It was scary, but it maybe felt good, too. "You heard me," he said sullenly.

Sebastian was silent for a moment. Oliver realized right then that he had no idea what his father might say. . . . "Oliver, what are you talking about?" Sebastian exclaimed. "Slay you? You're my son! Why would you even think such a thing? I would never . . ." For the first time in months, he reached over and ruffled Oliver's hair, then put his arm around him. "Come on, son. We can talk more on the way."

Stunned, Oliver allowed himself to be ushered along.

Oliver, keep talking.

And say what?

Say what you're FEELING already! Emalie sounded furious with him.

Oliver just wanted to keep moving . . . but he stopped and slipped out from under Sebastian's arm, because something still felt wrong. "You're lying."

Sebastian turned back to Oliver in surprise. "Excuse me?"

Now, Emalie urged. Oliver seemed to feel her opening the gate wide. "You're lying!" Oliver shouted. "I *know* you are, Dad!"

"Oliver —"

"No! I know about seventh moon, about the night of sacrifice. I know that Half-Light is making you slay me to show your loyalty!" Sebastian stepped toward him, but Oliver leaped back, slapping his hair out of his glowing eyes. "You're going to slay me with that Stiletto because I'm a failure!"

"No —"

"Yes! I am. And you won't say it but I *know* you think so! You don't even *talk* to me since you saw me with Emalie. I mean, come on, you guys know I still hang out with her. And what about all the doctor's visits? You *know* I'm screwed up inside and you're going to slay me and try again! I heard you and I know you are!"

Oliver couldn't believe the feeling of saying these things. And yet Sebastian's face remained impassive. There was nothing there. *Because I'm right,* Oliver thought miserably. And so he yelled on at his frozen father: "You don't understand what it's like to be me and you don't even care!"

Finally, Sebastian's brow narrowed. "Oliver, stop it."

"No! Just tell me! Or just slay me here! Whatever! I never wanted your stupid prophecy!" Oliver couldn't control himself anymore. He felt like he was sitting back watching this all come out. All the tight feelings of worry and frustration were bursting apart, walls crumbling, all the lies crashing down upon one another — what would happen next? He had no idea and he didn't care. Something new . . . And Oliver kept shouting. "If I'm such a failure, then just —"

"Oliver!" Sebastian lunged at him. His fist cocked back and shot out —

Everything went black.

< 156 >

CHAPTER 11

Transference

Oliver opened his eyes to see the moon. For a moment, his stunned brain leaped all the way back to Dr. Vincent's office. He felt a strange hope that he was about to find himself there, back in Seattle, maybe even back in December, when he'd known so little. . . .

Then he saw the frosted outlines of distant hills and the cold flashing of tiny lights. Fireflies, sinking and floating among the shocks of tall grass around him. He looked around and saw that he was sitting on a mountainside, in the moonlight. Above was the mouth of a cave, and above that, treeless rock scree led to the volcanic crater atop Mt. Morta. Its rim was frosted in bright moonlight. Below, meadows dropped down toward gentle, forested slopes. Far in the distance, Oliver could see the tiny bundle of lights at Fortuna and the branching roads. One road twisted right up the mountainside, ending not too far below their perch. Standing at the

< 157 >

road's end was an ancient stone castle, surrounded by a high wall.

"That's the Asylum Colony," said Sebastian. He was standing a few feet away, arms crossed, staring down at the castle. The wind made his coat flutter behind him.

Emalie . . . But Emalie was gone. Oliver remembered that she would have been forced out of his head when he was knocked out.

Now Oliver also remembered who had knocked him out and he started to push up to his feet, but his vision spotted with white and he collapsed back to the ground.

"Oliver, listen to me," said Sebastian, back still to him. "I had to calm you down." Oliver looked at him darkly. Sebastian seemed to be searching for words. "We're at the Asylum Colony to see an oracle named Selene. Half-Light has sent me to collect her life force. We need it to fulfill your prophecy."

Oliver stared at him. "Why should I believe you?"

"Oliver, I wouldn't lie to you."

"Yes —"

Sebastian turned. "No. Ollie, your mother and I love you. There are times when we don't *tell* you certain things. It's complicated, or it feels that way. . . . I guess we've made a mistake not talking to you more about your prophecy, but it's — it's because we don't know exactly what to say. We kept it a secret from you for your childhood so that you wouldn't feel overwhelmed. We wanted you to have a normal existence for as long as you could. But then when you started having trouble sleeping and all that . . ."

Oliver wondered if by *all that* Sebastian was referring to Emalie.

"We should have told you sooner," Sebastian finished. "Parents don't always know what to do."

"Why didn't you just tell me that?" Oliver muttered.

"Well, I suppose you're right. We should have talked to you as soon as we noticed your troubles, and well before you ended up befriending a human. . . . I can see how you'd want to get back at us."

Oliver just shrugged. He'd never thought of Emalie as a way of getting back at his parents. That was definitely not the case, but he wasn't going to point that out right now.

"Still, if I'd known that you thought we were going to slay you . . ." Sebastian sighed. "Oliver, we would never."

Oliver nodded. He found that maybe he believed his dad about that, and realized that this was also the first time they had ever talked about the prophecy, about Oliver's destiny. Still, he wondered aloud: "But the prophecy is more important than me, right?"

Sebastian looked away and Oliver didn't think he would reply. "To some people, but not to us. Do you understand that?"

"I guess. . . . So, you need Selene's life force . . . that means you're going to kill her?"

"Yes."

"Do you know why *I* was looking for Selene?"

"I'd guess that you wanted to hear your prophecy for yourself."

"Yeah."

"Well then, I think it's time you did. That's why I brought you along when I ran into you." He stood and offered a hand. "Come on, son."

Oliver looked at it for a moment. Could he trust his dad? Maybe. He took his father's hand, feeling the strong, firm grasp around his. As he stood, he felt as if those rushing questions that had overwhelmed him before had quieted. Emalie would have been proud of him —

Emalie . . . his dad definitely didn't approve of that. So there were some things that still needed to be worked out.

"This way," said Sebastian, starting down the mountainside.

Oliver walked beside him. "So, that Stiletto is for killing Selene?"

"Yes. The Stiletto of Alamut." Sebastian explained, "Tyrus retrieved it personally from the fortress in Iran. It was forged by ancient assassins."

"Why do you need Selene's life force?"

Sebastian patted Oliver on the back. "Here's yet another thing I should have told you by now. An important part of your destiny is coming up soon. You're going to be given extra power, by an Erebus demon named Vyette. This is why you've had all those doctor's visits. Dr. Vincent has been preparing your body to take on this power."

"What kind of power?" Oliver asked nervously.

"Well, I can explain it more later, but it will help you to meld with Illisius, when the time comes for you to open the Gate. But in order to summon Vyette, we need something called the Artifact. Actually, the Artifact is going to be retrieved on Isla Necrata. And in order to open the Artifact, we need Selene's life force. Did you follow all that?"

"Sort of," Oliver said dully. None of it sounded fun to him, to say the least, but then again, it was better than what he'd thought the Stiletto was to be used for. "But —"

"Hold on," said Sebastian. They had reached an iron gate in the castle wall. Sebastian approached a keypad beside it and typed in a code. The gate swung open.

Inside, they found a grassy courtyard dotted with trees. White light glowed from within the castle windows, which had been updated with modern glass. The lamp-posts along the walkways were lit with gaslights.

Oliver and Sebastian turned toward the sound of squeaking wheels. A white-clad orderly appeared, pushing a patient in a wheelchair past them.

"Good evening," he said. The orderly was a middle-aged vampire with slicked black hair. The patient was an older man. As they passed, Oliver sniffed the air.

"He's human."

Sebastian smiled. "Ollie, all the patients in the Asylum Colony are humans."

Oliver was surprised by this. "Really? Even Selene?"

"That's the point of the Asylum," Sebastian explained. "It's a cover. What humans think of as insanity is sometimes just the awareness, in a human, of the larger universe. A human can't fully grasp the concept of all the worlds and forces. Their short-lived minds try to understand it, but they can't. There are some specially touched humans, though, who become aware enough that they can act as oracles and are useful to the vampire world. We think that it has something to do with demon bloodlines that run through humans. There are other theories, too."

Oliver thought that sounded a lot like the Orani, except for the insanity part, although Oliver didn't

< 162 >

know whether or not any Orani had been driven insane by their abilities. He wondered if his dad knew about the Orani and found himself hoping that he didn't. "So the most important prophecies in the world are given by humans?"

"Yes. There was an old human playwright named Shakespeare," Sebastian continued. "Given how many plays he wrote and how excellent he was, you can guess that he was more than just a human. . . . Anyway, his plays sometimes included a fool or idiot who was actually incredibly wise, only no one knew it. Same with the people here.

"Humans would never recognize one of their own who had gained universal power, like an oracle, and they would likely lock her away as a lunatic, or shun her to the point where she would descend into crime and end up rotting in a jail. We arrange to have patients who fit the profile transferred to this facility, where we can study their power. The meeting of a human mind and a true awareness of the universe is a fascinating display. They can see things about the future that others can't."

"Like about my destiny," added Oliver.

"Exactly."

Oliver and Sebastian reached the front door, which was made of thick metal. Sebastian pressed a red button and a chime sounded. Moments later, the door swung inward and a gaunt woman in a white coat appeared.

"Good evening," she said. "Can I help you?"

"Sebastian Nocturne. I'm here from the Half-Light Consortium. Mr. Ravonovich's orders. Dr. Constance should be expecting me."

"I'm Dr. Constance," the woman replied curtly, "and I am expecting you. That's why I answered the door."

"Apologies," said Sebastian.

Dr. Constance let them through a short archway and into a wide entry room. A staircase arced up the back wall to a landing above. The high stone walls were decorated with medieval paintings. A suit of armor stood on display. Halls led off at every angle, only they had been fitted with steel doors and keypads. "So, you've come to see Selene."

"That's right."

"Well, I'm afraid I have some bad news."

"What —"

"The news is," a voice growled from behind them, "you're not going to be able to see her."

Oliver and Sebastian turned to find Uncle Ember standing in the doorway with two other vampires, leering menacingly.

"Excuse me, can I help you?" Dr. Constance asked.

"Yes," said Ember calmly, aiming a thin smile at the doctor. "Leave quietly and let us do what we came here to do."

"Which is what, Ember?" Sebastian asked gravely.

"Stop you, stop Half-Light." Ember cast a wicked glance at Oliver. "Stop this whole wretched prophecy. Now, that happens one of two ways. The first is that you and your son can walk right out this door and head back to Morosia."

"Well then, I guess it will have to be the second," Sebastian countered calmly.

"If that's your decision . . ." Ember's eyes burned emerald green.

Sebastian glared back at him and shrugged his shoulders. "Why, Ember? Just tell me why we shouldn't fulfill the prophecy. And don't say it's because you want to keep things the way they've always been. The only thing that's *always been* is change. We change. We evolve."

"Stop talking like a *human*!" Ember growled.

Oliver shuddered. Emalie had said the same thing to him once, right after Dean had died. He couldn't believe he was hearing it said to Sebastian, and by a vampire no less.

Sebastian shook his head. "Thanks, Ember, we'll be on our way." He turned to go —

With a searing hiss, Ember leaped, slamming into Sebastian. They sprawled across the floor.

Dr. Constance evanesced into a column of black smoke and slithered to safety at the top of the staircase.

Oliver watched as Sebastian flipped Ember off of him, sending him toppling into a stone column. The other two vampires started toward him. Oliver lunged and shoved one of them, surprising him and sending him crashing to the floor. Before Oliver could even set his feet, though, the other vampire had grabbed him by the throat and tossed him easily across the room. He smashed into the suit of armor and crumpled to the floor in a pile of metal.

Looking up dazedly, Oliver watched as Sebastian traded blows with one of the vampires, then spun and kicked him into Ember. Sebastian then leaped up onto the wall. He held out his hands, one fist beside the other, and a column of smoke grew out from them. "*Tachesssss*," he whispered, and his Naginata stick appeared. It was a long pole with a curved silver blade at one end that was carved like a falcon.

Ember regarded this with a snarl. He turned to one of the vampires and pointed at Oliver. "Get that out of here!" Then he turned back to Sebastian. "Pathetic," he growled.

"Really?" Sebastian replied. He launched off the wall, his long coat flying, the stick spinning in his hands. He landed and had cracked Ember across the chin before he could even move. But the second vampire landed a vicious blow, and the three descended into chaos.

An alarm began to sound. A far door burst open and two security guards rushed in, trying to pull the fighters apart and quickly getting sucked into the conflict.

Oliver scrambled to his feet as the third vampire ran toward him. He leaped away, arcing across the room and landing halfway up the staircase.

"Oliver." He looked up to see Dr. Constance at the top of the stairs, waving to him. Oliver bounded up to her. She peered at him. "You're the child of Selene's prophecy."

"Yeah," Oliver replied.

Dr. Constance pulled a key card from her coat pocket and thrust it toward him. "Down that hall." She pointed across the landing. "Room 209. Maybe she'll show herself for you."

"What's that mean?" Oliver asked.

"Just go," the doctor said, pushing him along. She turned and squared her shoulders, ready to greet Oliver's pursuer.

Oliver ran across the landing, trying to ignore the furious fighting below. Sebastian would be fine. . . .

He reached the steel door and swiped the key into a slot beside it. A beep sounded and locks unclicked in the wall. Oliver pushed through, slamming the door behind him.

More metal doors were set into archways along the stone hall. He checked the numbers and was passing an open window when it suddenly smashed inward, glass showering onto the floor. Oliver jumped back, then turned to see a blotchy hand grasping the window frame. The hand stuck right on a tooth of glass and yanked away. "Guh!"

Oliver leaned out the window to see Dean dangling precariously from the wall, Emalie hanging from his back. Dean smiled, relieved. "Little help?"

Oliver reached out and took Emalie's hand, lifting her through the window. He glanced back at Dean. "I didn't need help when *I* was carrying her," he quipped.

Dean rolled his eyes. "Look at me: I'm Oliver, I'm freakin' Romeo!" He hauled himself through the window, then frowned at the deep hole in his hand. "Remind me to pack this with dry dirt when I get outside," he said, referring to the zombie method of keeping wounds free of infection.

"We took the next elevator," Emalie explained as they started down the hall. "I could keep track of you until your dad knocked you out. . . . That must have been awful."

"Not really." Oliver shrugged. "He was just calming me down. Then we talked about the prophecy and Selene and stuff."

"Emalie said you let him have it," Dean commented.

"Yeah," Oliver replied. He glanced at Emalie. "Thanks," he said softly.

She smiled. "Don't mention it. Anyway, it wasn't hard to find you once we got out of the tunnel and saw this place."

Oliver stopped at the door marked 209. "Ready?" he said.

Emalie's smile had disappeared, and her face had paled. Oliver wondered what she was expecting in here. He swiped the key card, and the door to Selene's room clicked open.

They stepped inside to find it dark. Emalie flicked a light switch on the wall, and a single lamp illuminated. The walls were cream colored, bare except for one painting of flowers in a vase. An old television stood atop a metal cart with a chipped gold finish. The smell of the room reminded Oliver of years ago, when he'd met Sebastian's mother, Tally, who had been almost six hundred, with her skin almost gone, her dry bones and hair spray . . . Oliver also felt fear in this room: fear of death, of the end and the unknown. . . .

The bed was crisply made with white sheets and a brown blanket. Atop it lay an elderly woman, not moving. She wore a long, light blue nightgown. Her hands were lined with blue veins that seemed to be barely covered by skin. She looked so frail. How could something so delicate contain something as powerful as an oracle?

The three cautiously stepped toward her.

"So this is Selene?" Dean asked.

"Yeah," Emalie replied. As they looked over the old woman, there was a very slight chiming sound. Something moved in the corner, and now a tan cat peeked out from behind an old tweed chair. It meowed softly, and a tiny bell hung around its neck rang. Now a second cat's face appeared in the shadow behind the first, this one black. As the three approached the bed, the cats retreated out of sight.

Oliver examined the body. He could tell by her scent that Selene wasn't dead. But she wasn't breathing, either.

"Has she been sired?" asked Dean.

"No." Oliver couldn't figure it out. She wasn't in Staesys. "Dean, is there anything here we can't see?"

Dean peered around. "Nah, no magic going on here."

Emalie ran a finger along Selene's arm. "She's not here," she said, "but she hasn't been gone long." She looked around the room. "She doesn't like being gone, because she's afraid she'll never get back."

"How do you know?" Oliver asked.

"I can feel her emotions. It's her spirit, but more. . . . She's definitely alive, but she's left her body."

"Maybe it's transference," guessed Oliver. He'd heard of it. "It's like something between when Emalie goes into someone's head and when a vampire occupies an animal. You transfer your life force into something else, and usually you leave a summoning charm behind."

Emalie's brow furrowed like she was searching the silence. "She always longed to leave, but she knew it was safe here, until . . ."

"What?" Oliver asked.

Emalie looked at Oliver. "Until she realized that someone was going to kill her."

"That would be my dad," said Oliver.

Emalie shook her head. "She didn't go far, because there's something she still wants to do —"

"Um," interrupted Dean, "guys?" Dean had picked up a photo from the nightstand. The wooden frame was dented and chipped. Oliver and Emalie crowded around. The photo was stained, faded, black and white. Two women, one older, one younger, wearing plain white dresses, stood on the front step of a rickety wooden building. Sun gleamed brightly on their foreheads. The older woman had her arm around the younger in a motherly way. "So, that" — Dean pointed at the older woman and then glanced at the bed — "that's Selene. And we weren't in the museum for very long, but I think this other lady —"

"That's my mom," said Emalie quietly, "for real."

Dean flipped over the frame. He slid three metal tabs aside, removed the back, slipped the photo out, and handed it to Emalie. There was script handwriting on the back:

Selene and Phoebe, guardians of the Muse
Township of Arcana, March 14, 1868

Emalie flipped the photo back around, running her finger over it and staring hard at her mother's face.

"So," said Dean, "that's your mom, kinda, like, back in time."

"Seems to be," Emalie agreed.

"What's she doing there?"

"I have no idea," Emalie answered.

"I've heard of Arcana," said Oliver. "The Codex told me it was a town destroyed by Orani in . . . I think he said 1868."

"Orani would never destroy a town." Emalie frowned at the photo. "What are you doing, Mom?" She handed it back to Dean.

"Don't you want to keep it?" he asked.

"No, it's Selene's." She squinted, sensing the forces in the room. "She loves that photo."

Dean returned the photo to its frame.

The slamming of a door echoed from the hall. Footsteps hurried in their direction. "Ember said it was room 209!" one of the vampires called.

"Now what?" Emalie asked.

Oliver looked back at the frail body on the bed. *Where are you, Selene?* he wondered. Something soft brushed against his leg with a tinkling of a bell. Oliver looked down to see the tan cat. There was a blur of motion in the corner of his eye, and he saw that the black cat had leaped onto the bed and was curling up on Selene's legs, purring loudly. Oliver noticed now that the black cat didn't have a collar. . . .

Something else caught his gaze at the window, a tiny blinking light: a firefly. As he focused on the glass, he saw another, and another. . . .

He looked back at the black cat with its missing collar.

Footsteps neared the door.

"Guys," said Oliver. "I know where Selene hid herself."

"Where?" Dean asked.

"Come on," said Oliver. He crossed the room and pushed open the tall, double windows. "Hang on," he said. He threw an arm around Emalie's shoulders and leaped out into the night.

CHAPTER 12

The Temple of the Dead

As Oliver and Emalie landed in the grassy yard, Oliver heard the smashing of a door from above — and at the same time, the sound of frantic voices from around the side of the Asylum.

"Whoa!" shouted Dean as he landed. "They almost got me —"

"*Tsss,*" Oliver hissed. "Quiet."

He crept along the side of the castle until he could see the front gate. A collection of vampires walked briskly toward the front door. Their black coats with bone pins on the lapel identified them as Half-Light Consortium. Oliver recognized a few of them: Leah with her short frizzy hair; Yasmin in her head scarf; and Tyrus leading the team, his turtleneck high despite the warm night. "Leah, take the back," he ordered, and Leah started in Oliver's direction.

Oliver wondered for a moment if he should reveal himself to them. *Then you won't have a chance to talk to Selene on your own.* He found that, despite talking with his dad, Oliver wanted more than ever to talk to Selene on his own. And he was pretty sure that was what *she* wanted, too.

He turned and raced back to Dean and Emalie. "Let's go." They ran to the wall, Oliver grabbing Emalie again as they leaped over it and landed in the dry brush on the steep hillside.

"Where are we going?" asked Dean.

Oliver looked around. . . . There, up the mountainside, he saw one firefly, then another, and another. *Selene is best heard in the fires that burn cold. . . .* "This way."

Oliver led the way, scrambling among loose chunks of rock and tufts of dry grass that cast blue shadows in the light of seventh moon. As they hurried upward, the fireflies slowly gathered before them, in a loose order that vaguely drew a line up the hill.

They reached the crest of the mountainside and found themselves standing on the rim of a huge volcanic caldera. Steep walls of rock dropped hundreds of feet down into a crater where once a volcanic cinder cone would have been visible, but that now held the sparkling waters of Lake Naenia, the lake that was the spirit entry point to Hades' Well. The far side of the caldera ridge was much higher than where they stood, and its sharpest peak had been brushed lightly with snow.

Wind whipped at them. Oliver glanced back down at the Asylum, but couldn't tell if they were being pursued.

"There," said Emalie. Oliver followed her pointing hand. Just below the inside of the crater rim was a series of three flat plateaus, like steps down to the lake carved by a giant, littered with remnants of columns and walls. Oliver could see a small road winding away from it, through an entrance gate, and out through a cleft in the caldera wall. The plateaus blinked with meandering fireflies.

They would have to cross a steep incline of crumbled rock to get to it. Oliver led the way down, picking a path down the rock skree between large boulders.

"This is like skiing," said Dean. He started hopping, feet together, down the slope, only to start a slide of rocks. "Yah!" He tumbled, head over heels, down twenty feet. "I'm fine," he said, hopping up and limping badly.

They reached the first wide, rectangular plateau. A staircase led down to the next level, and then another to the third level, which overlooked the lake from atop a hundred-foot cliff. Some columns still stood to hold the temple's long-fallen ceilings, and some lay fractured into segments on the ground. The floor was mostly dirt and grass, yet here and there, sections of a smooth floor of white-and-rose marble peeked through. There was a plaque on the crumbled wall nearest to Oliver.

"Tempiale di Necromancy," Emalie read from the plaque.

"Necromancy?" Dean asked.

"It's when you speak to the dead to learn the future," said Emalie.

Oliver nodded. "It makes sense. Right beside the lake, with the Well draining out below it. Spirits will be passing by here and could be contacted before they leave."

"You mean like Emalie did with that security guard?"

"That," said Oliver, "and people probably listened to oracles here, too. Humans thought that oracles were being possessed by dead spirits. . . ." Oliver trailed off as green lights blinked past him.

The fireflies were congregating down on the lowest level, floating and falling like a fleet of tiny hot-air balloons. Oliver headed down the steps. On the final level, the center of each wall had a white statue of a woman, but the heads had long since crumbled away. They were likely statues of oracles in history. Two large, umbrella-shaped trees loomed over the plateau, one to each side.

In the center of the grassy floor was an exposed circle of shining marble. Oliver stepped onto it, and as soon as his sneakers slapped on its glassy surface, the fireflies all began to float toward him.

The marble showed some fragment of an ancient scene: what looked to be the wheels of a chariot or wagon, then three sets of feet, two in sandals facing away from the coach, and one set of bare feet, glowing golden, facing toward it. Below that, a Skrit symbol that Oliver didn't recognize had been carved:

Emalie and Dean spread out on either side of him, watching from outside the circle.

"What's going to happen?" Dean asked. Oliver looked over and shrugged. It was hard to even see Dean through the gathering fireflies. It was like Oliver was standing in a cloud of stars.

He reached into his pocket and removed the cat's collar that he had found on the statue of Phoebe in the museum, the one that was missing from the black cat in Selene's room. He held it out in his palm and said, "Selene."

He didn't really know if this was what he was supposed to do, or even if he was right in his theory: that Selene had transferred her energy to the fireflies, the *fires that burned cold*. But fireflies had pointed him to the museum brochure, which had led him to the statue and the Asylum, and then to the cat in Selene's room that was missing a collar. . . .

If he was right, then this collar was a summoning charm. When a being used transference, she would leave a charm behind in order to be contacted. All this, of course, assumed that Selene wanted to be found by Oliver, and he wasn't sure if —

"Oliver!" Emalie shouted. Her voice sounded like it was coming over a gathering wind.

Oliver looked up to see the fireflies beginning to swirl in a vortex above his outstretched hand, making a tornado of light that stretched up from the cat's collar into the trees above. They spun and gathered more tightly, until it was hard to make out the individual lights anymore; there was only the pale, green-white swirl.

"*Oliver.*" It was a woman's voice, the edges of her breathy voice buzzing with electric static.

"Selene?" Oliver asked.

"*Yes. I'm glad you found me. There is very little time left. My life is in grave danger.*"

"What do you mean?"

"*Your prophecy,*" Selene replied. "*Are you ready to know it?*"

For a moment, Oliver almost wanted to say *no*. . . . "Yes."

There was a sound on the wind like a deep inhalation. *"There will come a young demonless vampire who has garnered a power never before known among them, and who will at maturity be able to open the Nexia Gate.... The moment of choice will require a vessel so strong it can overcome the most powerful forces of the Architects. This triumph will free the* vampyr, *and establish a new order."*

Oliver ran it over in his head and felt a wave of disappointment. It was typically vague and prophecy-like, as far as telling him anything he didn't already know . . . "Is that it?"

"Isn't that enough?" Selene asked, as if Oliver was a slow student.

"What's that supposed to mean?"

"Oliver," said Selene, *"think. Freeing the* vampyr, *establishing a new order . . . Why can't you leave this world?"*

"Well, we're bound to mortal bodies, to matter. . . ."

"So to free your spirit demons . . ."

"I guess we'd have to destroy our bodies, and matter — oh . . ." Oliver felt a tremor as he understood what she was getting at. "By opening the Nexia Gate," Oliver said heavily, "I'm going to destroy this world."

"Yes. Nothing living shall survive the opening of the Nexia Gate," Selene explained. *"All matter will be*

returned to its primordial origins, to begin again. That is what the prophecy means by 'a new order.'"

Oliver glanced at Emalie and Dean. "They'll all be killed."

"Yes."

"But their spirits could survive. . . ."

"Perhaps, in some form, somewhere and somewhen in the infinite new worlds that form in the new order. But not as you know them. They and everyone they know and love, and every rock, and every insect, and even I will be destroyed, in the great reshuffling."

Oliver felt as if a bottomless pit had opened in his stomach. "Why did you want me to know this?"

"Because most of me is human. I don't want my world destroyed. My family is still out there somewhere. And as much as I dream some days of the end of my own life, to be free of this cursed power of 'sight,' to no longer be a prisoner of the vampires, what I dream of most is that the prophecy be undone."

"Is it possible?" Oliver asked, feeling a sudden flash of hope. "How?"

"Half-Light thinks that by killing me they are also insuring that the prophecy will be fulfilled, because a prophecy can only be untold by the oracle who told it. But there is another way. It has to do with the part of the prophecy about the moment of choice. . . ."

Oliver was distracted by a distant sound and turned to see Emalie shouting in his direction. Oliver peered at her through the vortex, but couldn't make out what she was saying. "What?" he shouted.

She pointed toward the stairs, and Oliver turned to see Sebastian bounding down the steps of the temple toward him, the thin steel Stiletto in his raised hand.

"*Quickly, you must release me!*" said Selene. "*Then hide the collar!*"

"But —" Oliver glanced at Sebastian. "You have to tell me how to undo the prophecy! What about the choice?" Oliver hadn't even asked about Emalie's mom yet. . . .

"*Please, Oliver . . . you can summon me again later!*"

"Okay, but . . ." Oliver hesitated. Would he have another chance?

Sebastian was almost to them, Stiletto raised. Oliver could hear him shouting now: "*Morchesss!*" It meant *death*.

"*Oliver!*" Selene cried.

"I release you —" Oliver shouted.

"*Aaaah!*" Selene screamed. There was a searing flash as Sebastian plunged the Stiletto into the fireflies. The scream tore at Oliver's ears —

Suddenly Dean slammed into Sebastian, knocking him to the ground. Selene's scream was cut off and the fireflies scattered wildly into the trees and rocks.

"Tsssss!" Oliver heard his father's cry and looked down to see Sebastian lying curled in pain and clutching at his ragged sleeve. Sebastian's hand and forearm were gone.

"Dad!" Oliver screamed.

Someone tapped him on the shoulder. Oliver turned to see Dean standing right beside him, staring at him blankly. "Wielders of chaos, guide my hand," he mumbled.

"What?" Oliver asked, his brain spinning. That phrase was familiar. . . . Oliver remembered Dean saying it on the ferry and seemed to remember hearing it somewhere else —

But he couldn't finish the thought, because Dean's fist slammed into his face.

Oliver felt a blinding crack in his jaw and his entire body was lifted into the air. He sprawled to the ground and watched, dazed, as Dean grabbed the cat's collar from his hand and ran off.

CHAPTER 13

A Master Revealed

"**O**liver?" He sat up to find Emalie running toward him through the few remaining fireflies. "Are you okay?"

"Where isshee?" Oliver slurred. His jaw seemed to be fractured. He got up and his head throbbed dully, but he shook it off. The jaw would heal soon enough.

"He — he ran that way," Emalie stammered, pointing up the hill. "Why would Dean —"

Unfortunately, Oliver thought he knew. "His master," said Oliver, "orders from his master." Oliver glanced up the slope, but then his eyes fell on his father, lying on the ground, his arm gone below the elbow. He rushed over as Sebastian slowly sat up. "Dad, are you all right?"

Sebastian's eyes glowed amber. "*Tsss* . . . I failed," he said, wincing and clambering to his feet. "Where is Selene?"

"Dean took the summoning charm," Oliver began, then paused, thinking, *Don't say any more,* but he went ahead and said it, anyway, realizing that another long lie was at its end: "I think he did it under orders from his master."

"His master . . ." Sebastian said distantly. Oliver expected the detached, disappointed gaze, but Sebastian nodded and gazed seriously up the hill. "You need to stop him. I'll —"

"Seb, are you down there?" Oliver recognized Tyrus's voice, calling from the top level of the temple.

Sebastian turned to Oliver. "Go, before they see you." Oliver saw something in Sebastian's eyes — was it uncertainty? Worry?

"Dad —"

"I'll be fine, Ollie. Go find Dean and get that charm back. I'll be along."

Oliver nodded. "Okay." There was entirely too much to sort out right now, but yes, getting Dean before he delivered Selene to his master: That made sense. And he *had* to talk to Selene again.

He and Emalie ran to the side wall and scrambled over. Ducking low, they started up the rocky slope toward the ridge.

"Did you hear all that back there?" Oliver asked.

"You mean the part about how you're going to end the world?" Emalie countered gravely. "Yeah, got that. But how could Dean do this?"

"He probably doesn't know what he's doing," said Oliver. "I should have seen it coming, but I just . . . He seemed so normal." Oliver wondered what else Dean might have done, secretly, at any point, under the sway of his master, and kicked himself for trusting Dean as much as he had. *You were stupid to just think of him as a friend. . . .* No! Oliver hated that thought. Dean was still his friend. *But can you trust him again?* He would worry about that later.

They reached the top of the caldera and were buffeted by the howling winds.

"Where now?" Emalie asked.

"Could be anywhere." Oliver sniffed the air, but the stiff breeze told him nothing. "Probably underground, though. Let's try the tunnel back to the Well."

They followed the up-and-down ridgeline until the shadow of the cave entrance came into view below. Scrambling to it, they headed into the tunnel. Here and there, a firefly blinked, almost like another bread-crumb trail for Oliver to follow.

Hurrying through the darkness, Oliver ran over what Selene had said. *I'm going to destroy the world,* he thought darkly, knowing it wasn't supposed to bother him. A normal vampire wouldn't have felt bad about that — maybe a little inconvenienced, but not bad. *Whatever,* Oliver thought. *I have to find out how to undo that prophecy.* Which meant getting the summoning charm back.

A scent finally registered. "Up ahead," said Oliver as they neared Hades' Well. "I can smell Dean, and . . ." Oliver trailed off. He smelled someone else familiar. Lilacs . . .

"What?" asked Emalie, noticing his perplexed face.

Oliver didn't reply, but held an arm out to stop her as they reached the end of the tunnel. They peered around the corner, onto the ringed platform surrounding the Well.

There was Dean, lying on his back, eyes closed. Kneeling over him in the eerie green light from the Well was a figure in a dark, hooded robe. The figure was whispering and checking Dean's hands, which appeared to be empty. Now the figure checked Dean's pockets, then his collar. The figure huffed and threw back the hood, revealing magenta hair.

Oliver frowned and stepped out onto the platform. "Lythia," he called.

Lythia looked up, momentarily surprised, but quickly smiling. "Hello, Oliver."

"That's Lythia?" Emalie asked, stepping out from behind him.

"Oooh, I heard about *that*," Lythia said, her eyes narrowing at Emalie. "Your human, right? You are the oddest thing, Oliver."

"I —"

Lythia cut him off, holding out her open hand. "So, where is it?"

"Where is what?"

"The summoning charm, silly. But of course you don't have it." Lythia's lips curled in a pout. She looked down at Dean. "And he doesn't have it. So who does?" She twisted around and peered across the platform.

As she did, Emalie gasped.

Oliver saw it, too. On Lythia's back, between her shoulder blades, a smoky impression shimmered over her cloak: a white handprint with clear dots at the fingertips.

"You're Dean's master!" Oliver said. He hadn't seen her from behind at the casino.

Lythia turned back, smiling broadly enough to reveal the points of her teeth. Then she gazed at Dean, shaking her head and clicking her tongue. "I should take this one back to the kennel and get another."

On the one hand, Oliver was struggling to put these new pieces together. Lythia had ordered Dean to take the summoning charm, and yet, here she was with him, but Dean didn't have it. So what had happened? On the other hand . . . "What do you want with Selene?"

Lythia laughed sweetly. "Silly Oliver. What did *you* want with Selene? As much information about the prophecy as you can get, I expect. That's what we want, too."

"Who's we?"

"Tut, tut, not telling . . . I . . ."

Lythia's smile suddenly faltered.

"Her father . . ." Emalie whispered. Oliver saw a red glow escaping from her closed eyes, and the scarab conduit charm in her hands. "He works for Half-Light. Malcolm LeRoux . . . They're after something called the Artifact, but that's not why Lythia wants the charm. . . . She has some plan of her own —"

"*Tsssss* — you!" Lythia hissed. Her eyes flared bright lavender and she thrust her hands out into the air in front of her, creating a shimmering wave of forces.

"Aahh!" Emalie was thrown back, landing hard, her head thudding on the floor.

"Stay out of my mind, you vermin!" Lythia's face contorted in rage and she leaped, arcing across the room, aiming straight for Emalie.

Oliver dove into her path. They slammed into each other and tumbled to the floor. Lythia writhed, getting her boots against Oliver's chest and launching back to her feet. She screamed in a venomous hiss, "Get off me, you useless waste of our kind! I'm going to eat your bratty little blood bag!"

Oliver jumped up, eyes igniting in amber. "You stay away from her." He lunged, shoving Lythia with both hands. She flew back, smashing through the stone railing, eyes wide. A smile began to form on her lips —

"Well, now" — until her back collided with the green flow of the spirits. There was an explosion of sparks and energy, making her body convulse and her eyes slide up into her head —

Yet then they snapped back, aflame in lavender, and she levitated back to the platform like a diving hawk. She crashed into Oliver and her fingernails raked across his shoulder, tearing through his shirt. Oliver toppled to the ground, Lythia pinning him with her forearm across his neck.

"*Tssss*," she hissed at him, then suddenly smiled. "You're cute, you know," she said devilishly. "If you want to keep it that way, don't follow me." She vaulted off him, landing on her feet with a sharp clack of her black boots, and glanced from Dean to Emalie. "You've got enough of a mess on your hands, anyway, don't you?" Lythia dusted off her cloak. "Till next time, Oliver Nocturne." She turned and started striding across the platform.

Oliver slid to his knees, then to his feet, preparing to jump. This wasn't over yet. . . .

Lythia's hand whipped out behind her, the fingers flying open, and her winnings from the casino scattered across the floor. Oliver froze as his brain helplessly began counting the teeth.

"Have fun!" Lythia called without looking back, and

she dissolved into a column of black smoke. Lythia could evanesce? Oliver barely had brain space to consider that, for someone who looked barely older than he did, she had a lot of power. The column of smoke slithered over the railing and down into the Well.

Oliver had counted the teeth in a moment, but Lythia was long gone.

He turned and rushed to Emalie. "Hey," he said, lifting her head. His fingers came away with a small smear of blood, and the scent of it made Oliver weak. *No.* He shook violently. *You are not that,* he scolded himself, but he still had to turn his head away as he lifted Emalie to a sitting position. She moaned groggily.

"Ow . . ."

"You all right?" Oliver asked.

"I don't like her. . . ." Emalie whispered.

"Oliver . . ." He heard footsteps beside him and turned to see Dean standing there, groggy himself, rubbing his head. "I —"

"Not now, Dean," Oliver muttered. He found himself wanting to yell at him, but resisted, keeping his gaze firmly away from Dean's. "Do you know what happened to the summoning charm?"

"No . . ." said Dean. "It's all fuzzy. I came out of the tunnel and somebody jumped me. Knocked me right out. I . . . I hit you, didn't I?"

"Yeah, well . . ." Oliver again had to suppress his anger. "We just met your master. Remember that girl from the casino?"

"Lythia? Really? Huh . . ."

"Mmm." Oliver didn't know what to make of it. Now he heard the whirring of the glass elevator, rising from below.

"Oliver." He turned to see his father emerging from the tunnel, walking slowly, the rags of his sleeve fluttering below the elbow. Sebastian glanced at Dean and Emalie in his usual quick, expressionless way, then his eyes bored into Oliver. "What happened?"

Oliver paused, realizing that he was about to tell his dad the truth, blow for blow, of what had just happened. How long had it been since he'd done that, without having to double-think about what he should and shouldn't say? "Dean's master was here," he began. "Her name is Lythia LeRoux —"

"Malcolm . . ." Sebastian growled. "Did she get the summoning charm?"

"No," Dean interjected. "Somebody got to me first. Hit me from behind."

Sebastian frowned, his brow knitting thoughts silently.

Behind them, the elevator doors slid open, and footsteps rushed out. "Oliver, Sebastian . . ." It was Phlox, in a burgundy velvet dress that fell to the floor. Some might have thought she was dressed for a formal event, but this was a traditional combat dress. In her hand she held a curved gold blade, a cursed katana sword, and she had painted dark black triangles back from her eyes to her hairline.

"It's all right, Phlox," said Sebastian.

Her face was steely, until she saw Sebastian's ruined sleeve and missing arm. Her eyes went wide, but not quite with the surprise that Oliver had been expecting to see. She didn't even ask what had happened. Instead, she said: "Did you —"

Sebastian shook his head tersely. "Almost, but no. Selene had used transference to hide. Oliver found her, but someone else has her summoning charm now."

Oliver could guess what this exchange between his parents meant. Remembering the conversation he'd overheard in Seattle, he understood now that, as the *"show of faith"* was Sebastian getting Selene's life force, maybe the *"sacrifice"* had meant the loss of his arm. They must have known that was a cost of wielding the Stiletto of Alamut, as enchanted weapons sometimes carried a price to the bearer. But Dr. Vincent would likely be able to regrow Sebastian's arm, so they hadn't been talking about making a new *son*, they'd been talking about a new *arm*. Thinking it all through now, Oliver felt great relief. He couldn't believe how wrong he'd been.

"Who has it?" Phlox asked.

"Malcolm LeRoux's daughter stole it, using her zombie servant." Sebastian nodded toward Dean.

Again, Oliver watched Phlox accept this with much less shock than he was expecting. Why didn't she seem surprised that Oliver wasn't Dean's master? Had they known all along? Suddenly that familiar, frustrating feeling of knowing very little of what was actually going on began to well up in him.

"Lythia?" Phlox asked. "But you said —"

"Lythia's working with someone else," Emalie suddenly said. Oliver realized that she was standing in plain sight, not hiding herself. And now he watched as Phlox and Sebastian actually turned to look at her. "We don't know who," Emalie added, her voice shaking slightly with the Nocturnes' eyes on her, "yet."

"Lythia didn't get the charm," Sebastian added. "Someone took it from Dean first."

Phlox looked to Oliver. "Are you all right?"

"Yeah," he replied, and saw relief on his mom's face. Phlox slid her katana sword into the leather sheath tied around her waist, then moved to Sebastian and put an arm around his shoulder. Oliver saw Sebastian lean in to her slightly, betraying how much his arm was hurting him. "Let's get you down below," she said.

"I don't know if I'll be welcome back at your parents'," Sebastian groaned.

Phlox moved him purposefully toward the elevator. "You mean Ember and his gang?" Phlox's eyes flared. "*Tsss.* Let him try to get in our way again. I'd enjoy the excuse. We're leaving for the boat in the evening, anyway. I doubt he'll show his face. . . ." Phlox sighed. "I can't wait to get out of here."

Oliver remained behind with Emalie and Dean as his parents stepped into the elevator. He wondered if they would even say —

"Oliver." Phlox and Sebastian were both looking at him. Phlox's face was blank, in that familiar way, but then she said, "Don't be long."

Oliver felt completely confused, but managed to nod. The elevator doors slid closed and his parents slipped out of sight.

Standing there, his parents' gazes fresh in his mind, Oliver understood that a great thing had just changed. Or, maybe it had been changing all along, and he just hadn't been able to see it. He thought all the way back to that night on the Space Needle, to the blank look when his father had first seen Oliver with Emalie and recognized the truth of their friendship. There had been that tense dinner, and Phlox's commanding words: *Get over it . . . over her . . .*

All spring into summer, even an hour ago when Sebastian had suggested that Oliver was using Emalie to get back at them, Oliver had assumed that his parents' silence and expressionless gazes meant the very same thing as his father's had atop the Space Needle: confusion, disappointment . . . feelings that had built up to the point that Oliver's parents had decided he was beyond hope. And maybe his parents' expressions had *looked* the same, but at some point, what those gazes *meant* had changed. What had once seemed like disapproval . . .

Had become acceptance.

It was all in what Phlox had just said: *Don't be long.* It assumed that Oliver would spend more time with Emalie and Dean. It accepted that these friends were a part of his life, and that maybe, at least for now, that was okay.

"We should get Emalie back," Dean said carefully, his tone still quiet with regret.

Oliver turned to them with his slight smile. "Yeah, let's go."

CHAPTER 14

The Boat to Isla Necrata

As Oliver, Emalie, and Dean walked up the tunnel, down the mountainside, and eventually into the sleeping streets of Fortuna, the three friends discussed what had just happened, making sure they had all the pieces straight.

"That's great that your parents aren't mad at you anymore," said Emalie, patting Oliver's shoulder.

"Kind of amazing," Oliver agreed.

"One problem, though," said Dean. "They still want you to fulfill the prophecy and open the Gate. And, well . . . you —"

"No," Oliver assured him, "I don't want to open it." For the moment, his anger at Dean's betrayal had faded. After all, it wasn't Dean's fault. And Dean was right: Oliver didn't want to destroy the world. So, the prophecy was a problem, but not for tonight. "We'll figure it out," he said, trying to sound hopeful, but inside he felt a deep tremor of worry. Could they? Selene had said there was a way to undo the prophecy, but Oliver wondered about that. He'd always heard that prophecies could not be undone. It was possible that he'd traded in his lies to his parents only to now begin a new lie to his friends.

Oliver looked up to find Emalie gazing at him oddly, almost as if she'd heard his thought. *Are you in here?* he thought worriedly. There was no reply. Oliver tapped his head and repeated aloud: "Are you in here?"

"Oh, nah. Not anymore," she replied. "That connection got broken when you were knocked out."

Oliver nodded, but at the same time he wondered whether or not to believe her. Emalie seemed to be able to get in whenever she wanted. "Well, so what's the odd look for?"

They had reached the inn where Emalie and her aunt Kathleen were staying. "It's just . . ." she began. "It must be a lot for you."

"You mean being responsible for the end of the world?" Oliver asked.

"Yeah, that," Emalie replied.

"Mmm." Oliver shrugged.

A silence passed over the trio. Somewhere up the street a door slammed. From the other direction came footsteps on cobblestone, the panting of a dog. The chirping birds seemed to grow louder, and a humming of distant cars grew.

"You guys should hit the sewers and get back down to Morosia," Emalie said. She reached out and hugged Oliver. "Have a good vacation. Be safe."

Oliver felt a momentary breakdown of his ability to think or speak, but then Emalie pulled away and hugged Dean as well. Oliver managed to say "Thanks," and "You too," and then, "When we get back, let us know what else you find out about your mom and the whole moon god thing."

"And that old photo," added Dean.

"Roger," Emalie said with a reluctant smile. "And we'll try to find out more about what Selene said, and how to save the world."

Oliver nodded. "Guess it's going to be a busy summer."

✸

"**W**e always have space," Myrandah said as she fluttered about the kitchen, "for a family that reconsiders their place near the sunlight."

"Right, Mother," said Phlox, busily arranging the Nocturnes' bags beside the door.

"But still Phloxiana refuses to see the dangers of the surface world," Myrandah grumbled disapprovingly, casting an accusing glance at Sebastian, whose arm was wrapped and tucked beneath a new coat. "I'd think you'd consider it for once."

Phlox spun and checked her watch with extra energy. "Wow, look at that. The boat leaves in two hours! Good-bye, Mother."

Oliver was joined at the doorway by Bane, who neither elbowed him nor made any sarcastic comments. Oliver had barely seen him since the museum. For once, it had been Bane who was already asleep when Oliver arrived home after dawn. Oliver looked up at him now and saw that Bane's face was strangely still. He was no doubt sad to be leaving his wild cousins and wilder times. Oliver thought about making some kind of obnoxious comment to Bane, something veiled and referring to unfinished business, something that told Bane that he knew that Bane was up to something, yet instead, he decided to enjoy this rare moment of silence and lack of punches.

Myrandah wrapped them both in hugs. "My darlings will be eternally welcome here, whether or not their parents approve."

"All right, Mother," Phlox said hurriedly. "We're off!"

"Hades' speed to you," Dominus called from the couch.

"Bye, Dad." Phlox rushed them out the door.

The Nocturnes made their way across the smoky city, down the entrance hall, and back across the ferry.

Rather than board the Charion, they proceeded, along with a handful of other families, down a passageway that ended at a narrow canal of normal, everyday water. A fleet of gondolas awaited them, each with a zombie driver. They pushed off and floated through an arched stone tunnel: an ancient Roman aqueduct. An hour passed, then slowly the scent of the water soured with salt and brine, and the Nocturnes' gondola emerged from the tunnel into a warm night.

Their faces were met by a stiff, salty breeze. On either side, high pads of grass created the walls of a salt marsh. The gondolas twisted among the grasses until they reached a dock. Distantly, surf could be heard breaking against a beach.

The Nocturnes walked up the dock to find themselves at the start of a wide wharf. A stream of black limousines hummed across the warped boards, each in turn pulling up to a steep gangway that led up to the deck of a small, amber-lit cruise ship: the boat to Isla Necrata.

Oliver felt a rush at seeing it. The vessel was a relic from the early 1900s. While it still had three red-painted smokestacks, its insides all ran on geo-electrical power from magmalight generators. Strings of golden globes arced from the decks to the front of the bow and along the railings atop the ship.

As they walked toward it, Oliver could hear the string quartet already playing on the lido deck above.

He could picture the open bars, serving frosted blood drinks in curvy glasses, with slices of passion fruit on the rim . . . the waiters passing by with trays of exotic Madagascar cockroaches, glazed with marzipan yet still alive and hissing . . . the swimming pools heated to boiling, smooth-skinned men and women lounging with their arms up on the sides, kids riding the nearby slides into the big pool . . .

All they had to do was climb that gangway, and for the next week, questions of prophecies and the future could be put on hold, and Oliver and Dean could just hang out. Sure, Dean wouldn't be allowed in the pools, given his zombie skin issues, but the two of them would have endless fun in the many casinos, in the video game lounge, the dance clubs. . . . And, Oliver thought, looking around at his parents, they might even have fun as a family. He saw that Phlox, Sebastian, even Bane seemed to be gazing at the ship to Isla Necrata as if it was a welcome sight.

It was amazing to have a thought like that — his family having fun together — but even given the questions still lurking, some things had changed for the better. Oliver no longer felt completely alone — maybe still a bit misunderstood, but not alone. And so maybe this would be a good week after all, now that Morosia was behind them —

"Seb!" The Nocturnes had just reached the start of the gangway, falling into line behind the other families and couples boarding. They all turned at once to see Tyrus walking quickly toward them, waving his hand. "Hold up!"

They stepped to the side of the gangway, letting the next groups of passengers on.

"Come on, let's go already!" Bane huffed.

"Quiet, Charles," said Phlox seriously.

"Tyrus," said Sebastian in his business tone. "Where are Ameilya and the kids —"

Tyrus reached them, and the dark expression on his face was clear in the amber light from the boat. "They'll be along. Listen, Seb —"

"What is it?" Phlox asked quietly.

"I'm afraid we have a problem." Tyrus's eyes moved past Sebastian —

"Gah!" Dean exclaimed. Oliver turned to see him toppling over —

Elbowed by Bane, who was sprinting away.

"Charles!" Phlox shouted. "What are you doing?"

Bane vaulted up onto the gangway, landing in a tangle among the boarding passengers, igniting a chorus of hisses. "Get out of my way!"

Now Oliver felt a rush of air. Tyrus had been joined by Leah, and they both stepped past the Nocturnes and leaped onto the gangway as well. They had their arms around Bane in a moment.

"Let go of me!" Bane shouted, thrashing around.

"Come on, boy," said Tyrus, "don't make this worse for your family." Tyrus and Leah leaped back down to the concrete, throwing Bane to the ground in a heap.

"Tyrus, what's going —" Sebastian began.

Tyrus looked at Sebastian gravely. "Sorry, Seb." He reached down, tore open Bane's denim jacket, and rummaged into the pockets.

Bane slapped and kicked in protest, sounding like a child. "Stop! Knock it off —" He landed a vicious punch to Tyrus's temple, but Tyrus barely flinched. Finally, he stood, tearing himself away from the struggling teen.

In Tyrus's hand was the cat's collar: the summoning charm for Selene. He held it up for the Nocturnes to see, then said everything he needed to say with a shrug of his eyebrows. Oliver couldn't believe it. Bane had intercepted Dean — taken the charm. . . . *Why?*

"Charles . . ." Phlox said faintly.

Lying on the ground, hair tousled, jacket torn at the shoulder, Bane's eyes glowed fiercely. "Give it back!"

"Silence!" Sebastian roared, and Bane cowered as Oliver had never seen.

Tires crunched on the sandy planks, and a limousine pulled up right beside the group. Leah stepped up to Sebastian and held out folded papers, her face cold and serious. "Half-Light has provided you Charion tickets home, leaving within the hour." Sebastian reached out and took them. Leah patted him on the shoulder with a pitying look. "Sorry."

"What now, Tyrus?" Sebastian asked quietly.

Tyrus glanced at the charm in his hand. "Everything continues according to plan. We summon Selene, acquire her life force, and raise the Artifact on Isla Necrata."

"What about us?" asked Phlox.

"You go home," said a thin, raspy voice from behind them. Oliver turned to see the limousine door open. A narrow face, ancient in the eyes, yet with smooth white skin, leaned out from the warm red light inside. "And you await further instructions."

"Mr. Ravonovich," Sebastian said apologetically, "I —"

"Just say you understand, old boy," said Ravonovich. "Better yet, say nothing at all."

Sebastian nodded.

Ravonovich smiled, revealing a mouthful of teeth, all of which were razor-pointed. "You know how these things go, Seb, Phlox . . . all works itself out in time, as it always has." He leaned back into the darkness.

"See ya, Seb," said Tyrus sympathetically.

Oliver watched him slip into the limousine, his hand stretching across the open doorway to give the charm to Ravonovich. He pulled the door closed, and just as he did, Oliver saw another head peek out from the warmth of the limo.

Lythia offered him a victorious smirk.

The limousine rolled away, rounding to take its position in the orderly line of cars dropping off passengers.

Oliver stood with his family and Dean beside the gangway. No one spoke as they watched one family, then the next, board the boat to Isla Necrata, excitement on their faces.

"Let's go," Phlox finally said. She took a step, then paused. "And Charles, if you stray, I'll chop your legs off. Do you hear me?"

Bane, his face ashen, got to his feet without reply.

Slowly, the Nocturnes made their way back across to the dock. A single gondola remained, waiting for them. As they reached it, the ship's deep horn sounded. They all turned and watched the golden-lit vessel ease away from the wharf, toward the moonlit ocean, the carefree days of fun, and the serious business of prophecies and the future — none of which would include Oliver and his family and friend. Oliver could sense the confusion and disappointment around him, and knew that, in many ways, things had just gone from bad to worse.

And yet, he didn't really feel like they had. At least for Oliver, all the worry and doubt seemed a little easier to deal with, now that he got to share at least some of it with his family.